THE CESSNA CAFE

THE CESSNA CAFE

CHINLE MILLER

Yellow Cat PUBLISHING

Cover by Cary Cox

For little Malcolm
And for my readers—some who may see their influence in this
book.

———

CONTENTS

1

Bud Shumway leaned against the old corrugated-metal equipment shed, watching as his part-time assistant, Kale, drove down the farm lane with the last truckload of melons from this year's harvest.

Harvest was always a time of mixed feelings for Bud, as he was happy to see the fruits of his labor go to market, but he also knew winter was just around the corner, though the warm day would make one think otherwise.

But before winter came autumn, Bud's favorite time of year when the desert cooled off, when the cottonwoods, tammies, and rabbitbrush turned gold, and when he was free of most of his responsibilities and could take the dogs and go explore the Big Empty, what Bud called that wide sweeping country around his hometown of Green River.

Winter would generally see him holed up in his and his wife's little bungalow or at her cafe, the Melon Rind, though some days he would be back here in the equipment shed fixing things. It would generally be a time to rest and catch up on things he enjoyed, like his photography, or to just help Wilma Jean with her cafe and bowling alley.

He could now hear the distant drone of an airplane, reminding him that things would be different this winter, as Wilma Jean had traded part of the bowling alley for a small plane, so Bud's help wouldn't be needed there like in years past.

He didn't generally like big changes, but the bowling alley thing was one he didn't mind—he was just happy his wife hadn't sold the Melon Rind, as that was his refuge on the days he needed to get out but when the weather wouldn't cooperate. His booth there in the back was almost a second home, where he would sit and drink coffee and watch the citizens and tourists of Green River come and go.

The plane was now overhead, and he could see that it was Vern Wells' silver and blue Cessna 150, the same plane in which Wilma Jean had learned to fly. Vern must be giving someone a lesson or even a flightseeing tour, Bud mused, Kale and the melon truck now long gone.

Soon, he could hear a second plane, and sure enough, it was a small yellow Piper Cub, and even though it was too high for him to see them, Bud knew it had black lightning bolts painted down both sides.

This was the plane his wife had traded part of the bowling alley to Vern for, and Bud wondered where she and Vern were now going. Probably taking tourists out to see the countryside, or maybe even doing some practice landings at some of the old backcountry strips like Hidden Splendor or Mexican Mountain.

Even though he didn't much like flying, Bud felt a moment of jealousy, wishing he had the drive and passion his wife had, as she was always out doing something interesting, whether it was learning to fly-fish or flying over the deep canyons of the San Rafael Swell.

He himself preferred more mellow enterprises, like wandering the backcountry taking photos, or even just reading about people wandering the backcountry taking photos.

He now wandered over to the nearby irrigation ditch, his two dogs, Hoppie, a Basset hound, and Pierre, a little black-and-tan dachshund, following at his heels, both playing in the water as Bud tossed them sticks.

He sat down under a big Fremont cottonwood that was probably a good 50 years older than him, which would make it near 90 or even 100. The thick trunk was corrugated like the tin equipment shed, with huge creases in the bark that helped hold the water so necessary to desert survival. Bud could see where its thick roots had pushed up from the dirt as the tree grew, roots that headed straight for the irrigation ditch. He wondered what it was like to be so grounded and to have such stability.

Now Hoppie and Pierre were back, dragging the sticks, dripping water and mud all over Bud's khaki pants and Herman Survivor boots. Bud threw the sticks, the dogs devotedly chasing them, half floating down the small ditch behind them.

Bud loved his life as manager of Krider's Melon Farm, though he occasionally missed his former position as county sheriff, but only when something interesting was going on, which really hadn't been that often. But he didn't miss the stress, as he'd basically been the only law enforcement in the area except for the state troopers, who had their own agendas to follow.

He'd finally convinced the mayor to let him hire a deputy, which had helped things some, and that deputy, Howard McPherson, had taken over as sheriff when Bud had resigned to go to work for Krider on the farm.

Howie had done a fine job, even though some Green River citizens had questioned his abilities at first, but he'd turned out to be a good sheriff, though Bud still had people tell him they missed him. That was no reflection on Howie, Bud thought, just the fact that Bud had been sheriff forever before that.

As Bud leaned against the big tree, musing on things past, he could feel himself gradually losing his native optimism and falling into a depression, something so totally unlike him that he wasn't even sure how to describe it. All he knew was that it wasn't a pleasant feeling.

The dogs were now back with the sticks yet again, proud of their catching abilities, and Bud felt that same pang of jealousy he'd felt a moment before while watching Wilma Jean flying through the wild blue yonder.

He wished he could be as carefree and innocent as the dogs, never worrying about where their next meal was coming from because they knew it would be Bud. If only he had someone so reliable to feed him every day with no worries.

He smiled a bit at the irony, as he knew he could always go to the Melon Rind any time he was hungry—he especially liked Wilma Jean's biscuits and gravy—but it was a fleeting moment, and his desultory mood quickly returned, coupled with a sense of poignancy that hit him like a freight train. What if this was the last time he would play stick with the dogs here?

Throwing the sticks yet again, he tried to get a grip on himself. He'd felt this way before, and not even all that long ago, back when Wilma Jean had talked about selling everything and becoming a pilot. It had felt like his world was being turned upside-down, though it had all worked out.

But this time, he wondered how things could possibly work out with this new twist of information that his boss, Professor Krider, a retired English professor from a small town in Texas, had just presented to him.

Krider was in that truck with Kale, riding along for the fun of it, as it would be the last harvest the professor would see, for Krider had just informed Bud that he was selling the farm, as his wife wanted to move back home to Texas—in fact, she was already gone.

Bud would soon be seeking employment elsewhere, an elsewhere that was hard to come by in a little town like Green River, Utah.

2

———————

Bud desperately wanted to talk to Wilma Jean, but he knew that was impossible, as she was currently high above the Big Empty, going who knows where.

His growling stomach told him it was lunch time, so he loaded the boys and headed home, where he would drop them off. Instead of having his usual soup and sandwich there, he would head for the Melon Rind Cafe, which felt even more like a place of refuge than usual.

He knew Howie's wife, Maureen, would be there, as she was now the manager, Wilma Jean having flown the coop. It was Friday, and meatloaf and mashed potatoes were always the Friday special, and maybe some comfort food would help stave off the feeling that his little drift boat had just been attacked by a longship of wild Vikings.

Bud was surprised when he got to the cafe, for there was a line coming out the door and the parking lot was full. This was a first, and Bud wondered what was going on. Standing in line at a cafe wasn't part of his small-town gestalt, so he kept going.

Maybe he could find Howie and moan to him about life's misfortunes, Bud thought, driving on down Green River Avenue toward the state park and Howie and Maureen's big farm house.

The state park was only partially full, so that wouldn't account for the cafe's instant popularity, Bud mused, noting also that it looked like there was no one at Howie's except their two Maine coon cats, Bodie and Tobie, sleeping in the big bay window. He knew Howie was probably out on patrol or at the office, but it had been worth a try.

As he rounded the corner by the railroad tracks, Bud was surprised to see a small crowd standing in the middle of the tracks, taking photos of the old historic railroad bridge just down the way.

They looked to be mostly middle-aged or older men, though there were a few women, and almost all were wearing blue baseball caps. A few wore striped coveralls that resembled what Bud wore when he was working on the tractor on the farm, as well as what railroad engineers wore, at least in the movies.

Bud wondered what was going on and if they realized they were trespassing. He knew this because back when he was sheriff, he himself had stood in the exact same place to get a photo of that exact same bridge and had been thoroughly chewed out by a railroad employee driving by, though the fellow had calmed down somewhat when he'd realized he was talking to the person he would have to call to make the arrest.

Now nearing the old art-deco station with the glass-block wall, Bud noted that the equally old Prickly Pear Hotel across the street had its *No Vacancy* sign flashing, a rarity for the somewhat decrepit three-story brick building. As far as Bud knew, the hotel hadn't been full since the days when Green River was a layover town for train passengers, sometime way back before the turn of the 20th century. The invention of the Pullman sleeper car in 1899 had really hurt the town's business, making overnight stops unnecessary.

Under the *No Vacancy* sign was a smaller sign lit up with the words, *Welcome Ragnarites*. Bud wondered what the heck a Ragnarite was, then forgot all about it as he saw Howie's patrol car down the road a ways, lights flashing.

As Bud got closer, he could see someone out in the road dragging something off to the side, and he then realized it was Howie, moving hay bales someone had accidentally dropped. Bud got out and helped as Howie looked relieved.

"Thanks, Sheriff," Howie said, still referring to Bud like he did when they'd worked together. "I'm sure not cut out to be a farmer, so it's nice to have one stop by exactly when needed."

Bud frowned. "I may not be one much longer, Howie."

Howie had bent over to pull hay stalks from his socks, so Bud wasn't sure he'd heard him.

"Hopefully when whoever dropped this gets home and sees half their load missing, they'll come back," Howie replied. "It's been a rough morning, Bud. I just got a call from the Beehive House and had to clear some things up."

"The Beehive House?" Bud asked, now sure Howie hadn't heard him. "You mean over in Loa? Why would you be involved in that? That's clear over in Wayne County."

"Well," Howie replied. "I know that, but when they called me, they said the sheriff over there wasn't responding, and the parties involved were from Green River and wanted me to take care of it."

Bud knew from experience that if a sheriff didn't respond right away, it was usually because they were busy—or didn't want to get involved in something they figured wasn't worth their involvement. He suspected this incident would probably be the latter.

"Take care of what?"

"Well, Mrs. Ames and Mr. Jacobs are both from here, and they got into a fight at the nursing home. It seems Mr. Jacobs was leaning into Mrs. Ames, and she whacked him. He fell on the floor and couldn't get back up. It caused a real ruckus, as everyone had to take sides, and they almost had a real-life riot, canes and crutches and such flying through the air. Seems even some of the nurses' aides got involved."

"And they called you?"

"Well, Bud, Mr. Jacobs wanted to talk to you, but when I told him you weren't sheriff anymore, he decided it was OK to talk to me. He wanted me to come arrest Mrs. Ames for assault."

Bud was having trouble remembering a Mr. Jacobs, as well as a Mrs. Ames.

Howie continued, "Mr. Jacobs used to run the old dairy just out of town, and Mrs. Ames was married to a Mr. Ames, who worked at the missile base."

Bud now vaguely remembered them. "What did you tell him, Howie?" He asked.

"Well, Sheriff, I gave him a lecture about being a gentleman around women. I said he should know better at his age, and I wasn't going to arrest her but would instead arrest him if he didn't apologize. That seemed to settle things, and last I heard, everything was back to normal."

Bud was now glad that Howie hadn't heard what he'd said about losing his job, as he was now reveling in living in Green River, where Sheriff Howie had things under control, even in nearby counties. He would worry about his job later.

"Looks like you'll have to start billing Wayne County for your services, Howie. You want to go have lunch at the Chow Down?"

"You bet," Howie replied. "I'll meet you there. But Bud, what's a Ragnarite?"

"I actually have no idea," Bud replied. "But with this town, you know we'll soon find out."

Bud had no idea how prophetic his words would be, nor that there would soon be more going on in his little town than he'd seen for a long time, and he would be right smack dab in the middle of it all.

3

Bud and Howie sat in a booth near the front of the Chow Down, waiting to place their orders. Karen, the owner, had already set hot cups of coffee in front of them without asking, made a comment about how they never came in anymore, then promptly disappeared into the kitchen.

The small cafe was filled to the brim, just like the coffee cups, and it seemed everyone was trying to talk over one another.

Toward the back, a small group of mostly men and a few women sat squeezed together at two tables, all wearing blue ball caps like the group Bud had seen on the tracks. He thought he could make out the words *Union Pacific* on the fronts.

Now a large fellow wearing pin-striped coveralls boomed out, "Am I the only one who misses cabooses?"

"Don't you mean cabeese?" A petite silver-haired woman next to him corrected. "And you know we do, you're just trying to get everyone riled up."

A man sitting across the table replied, "Now that's a stupid question, Billy. Of course we miss them! A silly battery box with a flashing light just don't have the same charm as a caboose. But you know that defect detectors were one reason the caboose wasn't needed any more."

A blonde woman wearing a pink t-shirt that read, *Loco Railfan,* said, "I've always wanted to buy one and make it into a cabin or something."

Now a young man who looked somewhat self-conscious said, "What's a defect detector? I think they should have a National Caboose Day where every train should have to pull a caboose just to prove they really used to exist. I've never even seen one."

An older fellow looked at him and moaned, "Gone is the mystique of the railroad man."

"Having no caboose is like reading a book with the last page gone," someone else chimed in.

Now a guy with a train tattoo on his arm said, "Actually, no, I don't miss cabooses. I like DPUs on the ends of trains better. Love the noise and power."

"You're just trying to cause trouble, Jackson," said Billy.

The young guy asked, "What's a DPU?"

Several looked on in mock shock as Billy answered, "You're new here, Robert, but you'll catch on. It's a diesel pusher unit. A regular old diesel train engine. And defect detectors can sense automatically when things are wrong, while the conductor used to stand by the train as it went by, looking for trouble, then hop in the caboose. Now the conductor rides in front with the engineer."

Now a sleepy-eyed guy who looked like he'd rather be in a caboose taking a nap said, "A train looks naked without a caboose. I'm a modeler, and thank goodness I have a whole fleet of little red cabooses. But I miss the old steam locomotives, too. Were they ever a wonder!"

The blonde woman replied, "Wait til you see Big Boy."

Bud figured the group were railroad chasers, as every once in awhile such a group would hit Green River. They were typically harmless, wandering around town waiting for trains, helping to put Green River on the map in their own way. He wondered who Big Boy was, but his attention was soon captured by a somewhat interesting-looking trio in a nearby booth under the *Today's Specials* sign.

He wasn't sure what they were talking about, but one in particular looked especially sullen, almost like he was about to punch the redheaded fellow across the booth from him.

"Nobody can even prove he existed," said the redhead.

"If you don't believe in him, how come you're a member?" the sullen-looking one asked. He had fair skin and blondish-white hair that hung down to his shoulders.

"I can believe, Bjorn, even though I know it's not true," the redhead answered.

Bjorn replied, "That's called cognitive dissonance, Erik. We're tired of you questioning everything. Why don't you just go on back home?"

The redheaded man named Erik looked hurt. "I believe, you know I do, or I wouldn't be here."

"You just said you didn't," Bjorn said.

"No, I said nobody can prove his existence, kind of like some religious figures, but that doesn't preclude you from having faith."

"Vikings don't operate on faith and belief. They're all action," Bjorn replied.

The third man sat silent, a pained look on his face. His reddish-blonde hair was tied in a pony tail, and he was so fair he almost looked like an albino. He and the one called Bjorn looked so much alike that Bud knew they had to be related.

Erik the redhead asked, "If Vikings don't operate on faith and belief, then why is not having faith a bad thing?"

Now the third man spoke. "Drop it, Erik, and you leave him be, Bjorn. If Erik hadn't paid for everything, we'd all be back in Podunk City. Sometimes I think you come along just to harass him, Bjorn."

"You know he deserves it, Sigurd. Somebody has to straighten out what his crooked grandfather did," Bjorn said.

"He wasn't crooked, and he didn't do anything," Erik replied testily. "Why don't you just let that one die?"

"I would love to see it dead," Bjorn scowled.

"We're just going in circles, as usual," Sigurd replied. "And as per the rules, this isn't stuff we discuss in public, you know that, Erik."

Erik replied, "Not much here in the way of a public. Just a bunch of..."

"Stuff it, Erik," interrupted Bjorn. "People of substance are listening." He nodded toward Howie, then Bud. "The sheriff's right there."

Bud casually pretended to still be studying the specials sign on the wall above the trio's booth. He turned to Howie and said in a rather loud voice, "I'm going to have today's special, Howie, how about you?"

"What is it?" Howie asked distractedly, still eavesdropping on the railfans.

Bud looked at the sign again. "Clam chowder with spam, spam, and spam. Actually, never mind, I'm having a hamburger."

He now pretended to study the menu, straining to hear, as the trio continued.

"I didn't do anything wrong," Erik protested. "You were the one who got arrested on our last sojourn, not me."

"You didn't do anything wrong *yet*," replied Bjorn.

Sigurd said, "Look, we all agreed to not argue and to stay under the radar, remember? By Loki." He raised his hand in a salute.

The other two looked irritated, but did likewise, replying in unison, "By Loki."

"Now lets go find something to pillage," Sigurd added. "I saw an ice-cream place around the corner."

The trio stood, paid their bill, and left.

Howie, his attention now back on board from the railroad conversation, said, "Man, Bud, I don't think Karen's coming back to take our order. This place is hectic. I'm getting a headache just trying to..."

"Eavesdrop on everyone at the same time?" Bud interrupted. "Me, too."

"I think we have some railfans in town," Howie replied. "I sure hope they don't cause any trouble, Sheriff. I mean, remember that time the train blocked the crossing and we couldn't get out to the airport?"

"That was the train's fault, Howie, not the fault of any railfans."

"I know, I was just remembering it, that's all," Howie replied. "That was back in the good old days when you were still sheriff."

Bud knew that Howie's neurons didn't always connect the way his own did, but he kind of enjoyed trying to follow Howie's trains of thought.

"I do sometimes miss being sheriff, Howie," he replied. "Things would be easier for me now 'cause you'd be a seasoned deputy. You were pretty green when you started."

Howie nodded in agreement, then looked somewhat somber. "You could always come back, Bud. Maureen and I just took back Howie's Drive In. The guy was over a year behind on his payments, and I'm not sure how we're going to run it, with Maureen managing the Melon Rind. If I only worked part-time for the sheriff's office, I think we could pull it off. And then there's the band..."

"You're not thinking of quitting law enforcement, are you?" Bud asked, surprised.

"No, but maybe go to part-time. You know, Bud, you'll always be sheriff, no matter what. But say, what did you mean by you might not be a farmer much longer?"

Bud was surprised. Howie had heard him after all, though it had apparently taken awhile to get from his ears to his brain.

"Krider's selling the farm," he replied.

Howie looked shocked, but before he could say a word, Karen arrived to take their order.

4

Bud had stopped by the house and picked up the boys, then decided to go back out to the farm. There wasn't that much to do for the day, but the house seemed empty, with no sign of Wilma Jean, and he wanted to enjoy his last days as a farmer, especially the part where he sat under the big cottonwood.

He knew Krider was on his way back to Texas, his wife and daughters already there. The professor had said all along that he'd wanted to try farming, that it had been a dream since he was a kid, and that once he'd given it a shot, he would probably go back home and enjoy being retired.

Bud had known all along that this was a future possibility, but he'd figured things might last considerably longer, since Krider seemed to like Green River. But the prof seemed almost as eager to return back to his hometown as did his family.

Roots run deep, Bud mused, again sitting under the big tree, trying not to feel too morose. He wished he could talk to his wife, for Wilma Jean could always cheer him up, even in the direst of circumstances, though he really hadn't experienced anything very dire to date.

He began fiddling with a small stick, rolling it in his fingers. His fiddling drove Wilma Jean crazy, so he tried to keep it on the sly, fiddling with things like rocks and rabbits' feet and the occasional diamond (he still couldn't believe that one), things he could hide in his pocket while fiddling so as to not irritate her.

But he seemed to have run out of things to fiddle with lately, and maybe that was part of the problem. It wasn't a matter of just missing having something to fiddle with, he *needed* to fiddle, it was a necessity, as it always helped him think, even though he had no idea why.

He immediately felt better, vowing to find a new permanent fiddling device, even if just a smooth rock. And shoots, if fiddling helped him feel better, what could be wrong with it?

He stood and walked over to the headgate. Irrigation was over for the season, so he turned the wheel that closed things down, ending the stick-chasing games.

He then wandered over by the nearby county road where he thought he'd seen some wild asparagus growing along the ditch. He'd pick some for dinner, which he knew would make his wife happy, as she was always trying to get him to eat healthier.

He realized it was too late in the season and that what he'd seen was the stalks gone to seed. He then saw something shiny in the borrow ditch by the road. Picking it up and scraping off the dirt, he realized he'd found someone's baton, probably some high-school twirler or even the band's drum major. He took the baton back over to the irrigation ditch, dipping it into what water was left and cleaning it up.

The baton was rusted and beat up, Bud noted, and looked like it had been in the elements for some time. Whoever had lost it had probably grown up and gone on to better things, like being a drum major at college, or maybe even something *really* big, like a drum major at Disneyland.

Bud now placed the baton between his fingers and slowly began twirling it like he'd seen the majorettes do while leading the high-school band in the Melon Days Parade.

It didn't take long to get the hang of it, and he soon had Hoppie and Pierre trying to catch the ends as he twirled it round and round, the dogs jumping and barking madly at this new game, making Bud realize how intellectually boring it must get chasing sticks all the time.

He tried to throw it into the air and catch it, but that was a bust, as it almost hit Hoppie on its way into the ditch. Pulling it back out, Bud decided he needed to try these more advanced moves when the dogs weren't around.

Suddenly, he felt elated. He'd found a cure for life's troubles, and this time, he wouldn't forget how much fiddling meant to his sense of well-being. The baton was a huge step upwards, a sort of industrial level of fiddling, one that he would never be able to hide from Wilma Jean, and maybe that was a good thing.

Maybe it was time for her to acknowledge that he was who he was, that fiddling was a part of his life. He would come out of the fiddling closet and no longer be afraid to be himself. It was a new day, and if people couldn't accept him, he'd just have to accept that they couldn't accept him and keep on living.

He could feel his baton abilities rapidly improving, even though he'd almost conked the dogs and himself a few times, and he now began twirling around as he twirled the baton, sort of an artistic statement on human circularity inside Earth's cycles, Bud thought, or even on Howie's sometimes circular synapses.

Bud quickly stopped, catching something from the corner of his eye, something pink. Someone was standing by his old Toyota FJ, someone he might actually recognize if only his head would stop spinning.

It was Wilma Jean, and she was laughing so hard Bud thought she was going to fall over, but she managed to catch hold of the FJ's side mirror and steady herself just in time. Her big pink Mary Kay Lincoln Continental was parked nearby.

Bud could feel his face beginning to turn red, but then thinking back to coming out of the fiddling closet, he decided to go hog wild. He began jumping up and down while twirling and going in circles.

The dogs got even more excited, barking and jumping, and Bud finally collapsed into a heap, puffing, as they piled onto him.

Wilma Jean caught her breath and said, "Bud Shumway, to think I thought you actually *worked* out here..."

Bud stood, pushing the dogs away and brushing himself off. "It's part of my new exercise program," he said.

"Hon, why do you need an exercise program? Don't you get enough exercise working out here all day?"

"I usually do," Bud replied quietly, still breathing hard.

He slowly walked over and put his arm around her shoulders, saying, "I need to find some other way to stay in shape, now that Krider's selling the farm."

"Oh, no!" Wilma Jean replied. "Bud, I just signed a loan for a new plane. I knew I should've talked to you first, but Vern's friend was selling it, and he already had three offers, and Vern talked him into selling it to me, but we had to act fast. It was a really good deal. I traded the Piper Cub for part of it, and the owner agreed to carry the loan for the rest, since we're both Vern's friends. It's a Cessna 172, a four-passenger Skyhawk."

"Is that where you guys went today?" Bud asked.

"Yes, Vern went with me over to Grand Junction and checked it all over, then followed me back after we did a test flight. Oh, hon, it's a beauty, and wait til you see it after it's painted. I'm going to use it to start a flying catering business. I'm going to call it the *Cessna Cafe*. I'll fly catered food into wherever people want me to go, you know, back-country weddings and bar mitzvahs, rafters wanting ice cream, that kind of thing, and I'll specialize in air drops."

"Sounds great!" Bud replied. "Where's the plane now?"

"It's out at the airport. But how will we pay for it if you're not working? We'll need everything I make to stay alive without your farm money, at least until this catering business gets going."

Bud felt a knot in his stomach start to form, but as soon as he picked up the baton and began slowly twirling it, the feeling went away.

After a long silence, Wilma Jean finally said, "I don't think you're majorette material, hon, but I think I know what we need to do."

Bud recognized this tone of voice, a tone that held an almost superpower level of determination, the voice his wife used when nothing was going to stop her, no matter what.

Wilma Jean added, "We'll just have to sell the bungalow and buy the farm."

5

Bud poked around in their small barn, looking for a pair of pruners, wondering how so much could be happening without anything really happening. He wanted to trim back the old heritage rose bush that was slowly taking over the back fence, making it nearly impossible to open the back gate.

He tried not to look at the *For Sale by Owner* sign Wilma Jean had put in front of the house, and he thought back to just recently when she'd tried to sell the cafe and bowling alley. Maybe she just liked selling things and should become a real-estate agent, Bud mused, though she'd probably starve to death in Green River, where nobody ever moved, at least not house-wise.

Except Krider, Bud thought, wondering if he'd put the farm on the market yet. He suspected Wilma Jean had already talked to him, even though it had only been a few days since he'd left and he was maybe even still on his way back to Texas.

Bud was now trying to trim the rose bush, though it wasn't cooperating and his hands were getting beat up. He headed inside to get a pair of gloves, the dogs following him across the big grassy backyard.

Krider had contributed a lot to the town while he was here, Bud thought, donating to various charities and even helping the sheriff's department get a new vehicle. Bud thought back to when he was sheriff and would drive his old Bronco to check on things, as Howie would have the department's old Crown Victoria—when it ran, that is. Now the department had an almost new Toyota Land Cruiser, thanks to Krider and Bud's friend Doc Richardson.

Bud wondered if Howie would end up quitting his job as sheriff. It would be handy for Bud, as he knew the mayor would give him the job again, but he wasn't sure he was ready to go back to the stress and worry of it all.

Bud found his gloves, then decided to take a cup of coffee back out with him, so he started up the percolator pot, then took the vanilla-bean ice cream from the freezer. He would put a dollop in his coffee, eating a small bite from the carton while waiting for the coffee to brew.

He wondered how much Krider made each year from the farm. Even though Bud was manager, he never did any of the books, he simply ran the place, deciding what kind of melons to plant, which fields to let lie fallow, making sure the equipment was well-maintained, that sort of thing. He'd always liked not having to think about the financial end of things. He knew Krider had his retirement income from teaching, as well as income from writing mysteries, but Bud really had no idea how well-off the Kriders were, though he knew they did OK.

He dipped absentmindedly back into the carton of ice cream. If they did buy the farm through some kind of miracle, Wilma Jean could take care of the financials, Bud mused, as she was good at that kind of thing. This was part of what made them such a good team, he did the work and she did the books.

He now felt a bit guilty, taking another bite of ice cream, for she worked plenty hard, too, especially at the cafe. Maybe he should help with the farm books, if they got the place. He could broaden his horizons—it would be good to know how to do such things, though Bud really had little interest in credits and debits and pluses and minuses and all that. It was sometimes hard enough trying to figure out some of the technical stuff in his camera manual.

The coffee now ready, Bud put a dollop of ice cream into the cup and put the carton back in the freezer, noting he'd just eaten about a quarter of it. He frowned, wondering if he was going to someday turn into one of those old guys who did everything on automatic pilot, lost in the glow of days gone by.

Rose bush forgotten, Bud now carried his coffee cup into the living room and fired up the computer. He wanted to search the Internet and see what a Ragnarite was, though after a few minutes of that, he came up empty handed. He'd had a hunch that the trio in the Chow Down had something to do with the hotel sign and were up to no good, and he wouldn't mind knowing what kind of no good they were up to.

He had noticed that the *Welcome Ragnarites* sign was turned off when he'd driven back by the Prickly Pear Hotel on his way back to the farm. Maybe they'd already outworn their welcome, he thought.

Bud now began to wonder what it would be like to live in Krider's big farm house. He really didn't want to think about leaving the bungalow, the place he and Wilma Jean had slowly turned into a comfy refuge with its big shady yard under the old globe-willow tree with the little barn and views of the sweeping Bookcliffs, as well as the small Airstream trailer out under the flowering Catalpa trees by the back ditch.

Krider's house had been a typical old two-story farm house until Mrs. Krider had done a spectacular job of restoring it. Bud knew they'd spent a fortune sprucing up things like the old winding oak staircase and the stained-glass window in the foyer. She'd turned it into a showcase, a place much too nice for Bud, as he preferred not having to take his shoes off when he came in the door. He could recognize greatness when he saw it, but that didn't mean he wanted to live in it.

He was now wondering what the history of the farm was. All he knew was that it had once belonged to one of the Farrar brothers, early local businessmen. He searched on the words *Farrar Green River*, but found only some entries from a genealogical site and stuff about the old Palmer House, which they'd built and which had successfully competed with the Prickly Pear Hotel.

He now keyed in the address of Krider's farm plus *Farrar* to see what that might find. To his surprise, he found an old entry from a digitized copy of the *Times Dependent* newspaper down in Radium. It was dated 1930 and read:

Green River News
    by Laura Chandler
    Our last installment left you wondering what had become of Fannie McGregor after she sold the old Farrar place to a family from back East. She and Tom had bought the farm from the Farrars only a few years before Tom was tragically killed in a 1910 combine accident, leaving Fannie to fend for herself and her three young boys and two girls, trying to run a large farm with no man around to help. But she was successful, and each of her children grew up to successfully contribute to our Green River heritage.

    Fannie sold the farm to the Nelson family in 1929 and moved into town, where she bought a beautiful little Craftsman cottage. She loves to garden and is said to have the biggest and tastiest sweet peas in town.

    1910, incidentally, was the same year that the Midland Trail came through town, connecting Washington, D.C. to San Francisco and bringing the town's first motor tourists. And as you know, a flood in 1927 changed the course of the river, shifting it about three-quarters of a mile east to where it now lies.

    This shift greatly affected the McGregor Farm, flooding fields with a rich black loamy soil that makes the farm still one of the best producers in the area.

    Stay tuned next week for more on the old remnants of railroad worker houses from the late 1800s and how some locals have recently claimed to have seen Japanese ghosts in that area. Japanese workers were primarily responsible for building this section of the Denver and Rio Grande Railroad, and we'll go into why it wasn't the Chinese, who helped build many of our country's great rail lines.

    See you next week!

Bud shut down the computer, wondering if the Japanese ghosts were still around. What he'd read had been kind of interesting, especially the part about the farm being such a good producer, but he knew if he stayed online he would soon be going down deep rabbit holes, the kind even good rabbit dogs like Pierre and Hoppie couldn't help him out of.

He drank the last of his coffee, poured himself a new cup, put a dollop of ice cream in it, and went back outside.

6

Bud was turning onto the farm road, wondering where he'd left his baton, when his phone rang.

"Yell-ow," he answered.

"Sheriff, it's Howie. I need your help."

Bud waited for Howie to continue, wondering how many neural pathways a human brain could hold.

Finally, Howie said, "You there, Bud?"

"Here. Patiently waiting for more intel," Bud replied.

"Intel? What's intel?"

Bud sighed. "Howie, I'm waiting for more intelligence from you. It's an old Army term for information."

"Well, I was never in the Army, Bud, you know that," Howie replied, sounding irritated. "And there's no need to insult my intelligence. I don't know how you always manage to get me sidetracked when I have important information to relate."

Bud groaned, then decided it would be fruitless to tell Howie he hadn't been in the military either. He parked the FJ by the irrigation ditch, thinking he could see his baton next to the big cottonwood there. Bud let the dogs out, finding the baton where he'd left it, right under the big tree. He was soon twirling it, instantly feeling better, still holding the phone to his ear with his other hand.

Howie still hadn't said a word, and Bud thought he'd lost him, but he could now hear people talking in the background, and the voices sounded somewhat familiar.

"Where are you, Howie?"

Howie replied, "Oh, there you are. I thought you hung up. Sheriff, can you come down to the tracks near my house, by the old bridge? There's been an incident, and I need your help."

"An incident or an accident?" Bud asked, not quite sure what Howie had said.

"An incident. Bud, I need backup. We may have to stop a train or two. I'm waiting for the railroad people to show up, but who knows when that might be."

Stop a train or two? Bud sighed. He could tell Howie was somewhat discombobulated, and if he wanted to know more, he'd just have to go see for himself.

"I'll be right there, Howie," Bud said.

He loaded the dogs back into the FJ, tossed the baton onto the back seat, and headed for the railroad tracks, wondering what was going on.

He'd always told Howie to call if he needed help, but there had been times when Howie had called for what Bud had considered trivial matters, and he hoped this wasn't one of those times, as he really wanted to just hang around the farm some more and feel all poignant about losing his job. He wanted to fully enjoy the feeling, as it was easier than actually looking for a new job.

He was soon by the state park, then went by Howie's, noting again that Bodie and Tobie were sleeping in Howie's bay window, though this time Maureen's VW Bug was parked by the house.

That would mean Wilma Jean was at the cafe, Bud noted. Maybe he'd stop by there after seeing what Howie was up to and see if she'd had a chance to talk to Krider.

Bud was soon by the railroad tracks, where he parked next to the sheriff's Land Cruiser. It was just like the other day, a small crowd of people standing on the tracks near the old bridge, all wearing blue baseball caps, and he wondered if he hadn't somehow double-clutched it and gone back in time.

Howie was on his knees, examining something on the tracks as the crowd excitedly exchanged ideas on what had transpired. Bud recognized a few from lunch at the Chow Down.

"See, here you can actually see the marks from the pry bar," said the man that Bud thought had been called Billy.

The rookie railfan named Robert was scratching his head, trying to make sense of it all. He asked, "Wouldn't it be hard to pry up a piece of track like that? I see heavy railroad equipment doing these jobs, so how could one person do it? Maybe they used dynamite."

"Don't be silly," the silver-haired woman said. "Billy just showed you the crowbar tracks. A strong man could pry the thing up. You pry off the spike, then the clutch, then you can pry the rail out of place. The real question is, why would anyone want to?"

"I love trains. always have, always will," said an old-timer, apparently enjoying the show, though maybe not fully aware of what was going on.

"I love trains, too," said another. "And firetrucks."

Now Howie, seeing Bud, motioned for him to come over. Billy, who Bud had decided was the group leader of some sort or another, motioned for everyone to stand back, as if a detonation was imminent.

"Someone pried up a piece of the track, Sheriff," Howie informed him grimly. "These guys were out here taking photos and found it, or the next train would've been toast."

"Have you contacted the railroad, Howie? They need to stop any traffic coming this way."

"I did, Bud. They're on their way now. But who would do something like this? We get these big freight trains through here, as well as Amtrak. A lot of damage and lives could be lost from something like this. And the state park and my house aren't even that far away." Howie's voice trailed off with the thought.

"I don't know," Bud replied quietly. "It doesn't make sense."

"It does make sense," said Billy. "I'm Billy Belanger. I used to work for the D&RGW as a conductor. I think it has something to do with counting coup on Big Boy."

"Who's Big Boy?" Howie asked.

Billy shook his head. "No offense, Sheriff, but you sure don't keep track of the happenings around your own little town, do you?"

Now the silver-haired woman said, "Billy, Billy, Billy. You sure didn't win any ribbons in the tact contest, did you?"

Billy looked chagrined. "This is my mom, Dot," he explained. "She's right. To us railfans, getting to see Big Boy is the event of a lifetime. But the average Joe probably doesn't care all that much that the largest steam engine in history will be running through their town on its maiden run."

"Maiden run? They're still building steam engines?" Howie asked incredulously.

Billy laughed. "No, son, Union Pacific just finished restoring steam locomotive Big Boy No. 4014. I guess you're right, it's technically not its maiden run. They're taking it up to Ogden to a ceremony commemorating the anniversary of the Golden Spike. That was the last spike driven to complete the transcontinental railroad in 1869. I think somebody is trying to derail things."

"How could anyone not love a big old steam engine?" asked Dot. "The whistle brings tears to your eyes and Jimmie Rodgers to your ears."

"Maybe it's not Big Boy they don't like as much as Union Pacific," Billy replied. "That's a real flagship for them in the PR department, and they spent a lot of money restoring it."

Bud nodded, then said, "You deserve a big attaboy for finding this."

"My mom saw it first," said Billy.

"OK, a big attagirl," Bud corrected. "I just hope railroad dispatch has stopped all the trains."

"I sent a couple of guys in each direction to stop any trains coming through," Billy said. "Those big freights need a couple of miles to stop, so the guys went out a ways, and they're old railroad employees, so they know the signals to use."

"Did anyone see anybody messing around out here?" Howie asked.

"Not really," Billy replied. "But my mom here said she saw a fellow walking along the golf course not too long before we saw this, and he sure didn't look like he was playing golf."

"He was an albino," Dot said. "White hair and skin like a sheet, a white sheet, not one of those fancy Ralph Lauren ones with colors that make your eyeballs spin. An albino or a ghost, one or the other. And he looked guilty as all heck."

"Now, Mom, you weren't even close enough to see his expression, how could you know that?" Billy asked.

"William, I'm gonna bop you on the head if you don't quit being so condescending. He looked guilty because he was carrying a big old crowbar. I first thought it was a golf club with no end on it, but then I realized that nobody plays golf that way—they wouldn't get anywhere. Does that answer your question?"

Bud wasn't sure if she was talking to him or to Billy, so he just nodded his head in agreement.

"He dropped it when he saw I was watching him," Dot added. "Right over there by that big Russian olive."

Just then, a pickup with the words D&RGW on its door drove up. As Howie went to talk to the railroad man, Bud headed across the golf course, looking for the crowbar. He knew he needed to find it in case the man with white hair came back for it, as its fingerprints could be prime evidence, evidence that could possibly implicate the sullen-acting trio he'd seen in the Chow Down.

But it was not to be, for look as he may, there was nary a crowbar to be found anywhere on the Green River Golf Course.

7

It was almost dark, and Bud was gathering the pieces of rose bush from his earlier trimming, wondering how such a beautiful plant could be so painful. He wanted to get it done before the forecasted storm came in, and dark clouds already hung over the Reef.

He would've been done long ago if he hadn't spent such a long time looking for the crowbar the white-headed man had dropped on the golf course, he thought, a bit irritated.

It bothered him that he hadn't been able to find it, and all he could figure was that the man had been hiding in the bushes and had grabbed it while they'd been up on the tracks talking. The man had apparently panicked when he saw Dot watching him, but then, realizing he'd dropped a piece of incriminating evidence, had gone back for it.

After that, Bud had stopped by the Melon Rind, where he and Wilma Jean had a good talk back in the kitchen, since the place was still full. He had somewhat mournfully explained to his wife that he didn't want to leave the bungalow, that it was his home, and, like the fact that he was a consummate fiddler, it was part of who he was.

He told her that they should abandon the idea of buying Krider's farm, and he would just go back to being Howie's deputy, or even the sheriff, if Howie should ever quit. But he didn't belong in a fancy house with a polished oak staircase under a wall with small stained glass windows shaped like diamonds—it would all be wasted on him.

Wilma Jean had laughed a little, which had hurt Bud's feelings until he realized she was laughing from relief because she agreed with him.

She hadn't been able to get in touch with Krider anyway, as she'd been too busy with her new plane and catering business. She already had an air drop planned for the next day, and Sammy out at the airport had finished painting the Cessna just in time.

At that point, the cafe had gotten even busier, so Bud had come on home.

He took the for-sale sign down and was beginning to feel a little better, knowing they wouldn't be selling the bungalow. He could now go back to worrying about finding a job.

Now finished with the roses, Bud realized he'd been too worried to eat, so he went into the kitchen and fixed himself a bowl of cereal. After a few bites, he decided he wasn't hungry and gave it to the dogs.

Kicking back in his big recliner, he thought that maybe being worried and depressed was a good weight-loss strategy, though not a fun one. Maybe he could put off job hunting until he lost a few pounds and got down to where he wanted to be.

He could now hear distant thunder and got up and closed the windows, bringing Wilma Jean's petunias into the mud room in case it hailed, battening down the hatches.

It was supposed to rain all night and into the next day, and he wondered how Wilma Jean could possibly make an air drop in the rain. If it were windy, he knew she'd for sure be shut down, and he wondered if she'd taken bad weather into account when calculating how often she could potentially fly.

He hadn't spent much time thinking about her new business, as it had all happened so fast, but now that he had time to kick back, Bud began to question whether or not it was a good idea.

First, flying itself had a level of danger associated with it, for unlike when driving a car, one couldn't just pull over if you had engine failure. Wilma Jean hadn't had her license very long, and the kind of flying she'd be doing required flying low to the ground—not as low as a crop duster, maybe, but low enough that you could drop supplies without making the recipient have to duck or to take a hike to retrieve them. And on top of all this, she would be flying a plane that was new to her.

Bud now realized he had enough to worry about that he could probably go quite some time without having his appetite return. He could actually get skinny like he'd been back in high school.

And on top of all this, he was concerned that whoever had tried to derail a train might be back or have even bigger plans. According to Billy, Big Boy wasn't set to arrive for several more days, and he didn't know how Union Pacific or the Denver and Rio Grande Western could monitor miles and miles of tracks. Someone could easily pop another section of rail and maybe no one would be the wiser until a train wrecked. The Big Empty had miles of track just ripe for the pulling.

Little Pierre was now asleep on Bud's lap, snoring, and Hoppie was at his feet, also asleep, and Bud felt himself drifting off. He knew his wife wouldn't be home for several hours, for if Maureen had the day off, Wilma Jean would have to close up the cafe.

Bud again wondered what a Ragnarite was and, in an attempt to stay awake, decided to do one more Internet search, but this time, he would search on *Ragnar* instead of *Ragnarite*.

He instantly hit paydirt and wondered why he hadn't tried this earlier, as it was obviously someone's name.

Ragnar Lothbrok (Old Norse for Ragnar Shaggy Breeches) was a legendary Danish and Swedish Viking hero and ruler, known from Old Norse sagas.

Ragnar distinguished himself by many raids against France and Anglo-Saxon England during the 9th century. There is debate as to whether or not he actually existed.

According to the "Tale of Ragnar Lothbrok," Ragnar was the son of the Swedish king Sigurd Hring. Sigurd ruled Sweden and Denmark from

about 770 until his death in about 804. He was succeeded by Ragnar.
Harald Wartooth's son Eysteinn Beli ruled Sweden as Ragnar's viceroy
until he was killed by the sons of Ragnar.

The "Tale of Ragnar's Sons" tells that the Great Heathen Army that
invaded England in 865 was led by the sons of Ragnar to wreak revenge
against the King of Northumbria who had supposedly captured and
executed Ragnar.

Bud, now wide awake, shut the computer down and kicked back, thinking. So, apparently someone had started a Ragnarite club or something to honor this Viking fellow, Ragnar Shaggy Breeches—or maybe they were his descendants, though this might be tricky if Ragnar didn't really exist.

In any case, the trio at the Chow Down, assuming they were Ragnarites, did remind Bud a little of how he would picture Vikings —sullen and argumentative and having red and blonde hair and fair skin. In fact, now that he thought of it, the two white-haired guys looked to be Swedish, not albinos, but blonde and pale, as someone from Scandinavia could be. After all, Bud knew that people in the northern climes had adapted to the lack of sunlight by having pale skin and fair hair and blue eyes.

Bud hadn't been close enough to notice if they had blue eyes, but he did know that people with blue eyes were less likely to get SAD, or Seasonal Affective Disorder, as blue eyes took in more sunlight than any other color. Maybe he should research that, he thought, turning back to the computer.

Just in time to save him from getting lost in the aether, Bud's phone rang.

"Yell-ow," he answered.

It was Sammy, the airport manager.

"Bud, I can't get ahold of Howie or your wife. I came back over to the airport to turn on the night lights, and when I checked the hanger, I found that someone got into her new plane and maybe stole some stuff."

"Shoots, Sammy, what kind of stuff?" Bud asked.

"Well, she had an air drop planned for tomorrow, and it looks like they got into her supplies. There's stuff scattered all over the place. I just got the darn thing painted like she wanted, and they messed up the door. It looked like they used a crowbar to pry it open."

"Was the hanger locked up, Sammy?"

"No, Bud, I never lock it until night after I turn on the airport lights. I don't want to go giving keys out to anyone and their dog just because they might have a plane in here, 'cause sometimes it's just someone passing through, so I leave it open. I may have to rethink that."

"OK, thanks, Sammy. I'll be right out."

"I'll wait for you, Bud, 'cause I'll need to lock it up after you leave."

"I'll hurry, Sammy, and thanks."

Bud hung up the phone, grabbed his Ruger and its holster, then opened the door to leave, turned around and got his rain jacket, then headed out into the midst of a gully washer, wondering if Vikings had indeed come to Green River, and if so, why.

8

Bud swung into Howie's drive, where Howie waited in his Land Cruiser, lights flashing. Bud had decided he should take him along, since technically a crime had been committed, plus Bud didn't want to have to explain it all to him later.

He pulled up next to the Land Cruiser, motioning for Howie to roll down his window.

"It's raining, Bud," Howie complained, rolling his window half down.

"I can see that, Howie," Bud replied. "But you should ride with me. If the culprit's still out there, it's better to keep a low profile. Our chances of seeing him might improve."

Howie was soon in the FJ, soaking wet.

"Dang it, Bud, it's raining."

"I can see that, Howie," Bud said again, patiently.

"You would think someone would pick a nicer night to go rampaging around stealing things."

"They probably figured it would be OK, since they were inside a nice dry hanger."

"You think this is another crowbar incident, Bud?" Howie asked. "It sounded like it, the way you described it on the phone."

They'd crossed the tracks and were now on the road to the airport. It was raining so hard Bud would've missed the turnoff if he hadn't already known the way.

"It could be, Howie," Bud said. "Though who knows if it was the same crowbar or not. By the way, did the railroad detective ever show up?"

"He did, and he was a bit short with me, Sheriff."

"Oh, how so?"

"He said all those people around were destroying any possibility of finding any evidence. This was after I'd already pointed out the evidence—a gap in the line. Having Billy trying to tell him everything that had happened along with his mom and a couple of other railfans all at the same time didn't help much. One guy even started asking him what it was like to be a railroad detective and wanted a blow by blow of his life. The detective said he'd call me if he found anything of importance."

Bud nodded. He could now see that Sammy had turned on the airport lights, though they were barely visible through the rain. The Green River Airport was closed at night, but Sammy always turned the lights on in case some pilot had an emergency. Bud had never figured out how they would see the runway, since the lights only lit its end, but he guessed they could at least see where not to go.

Bud was now keeping an eye out for any sign of an intruder, though the rain made it hard to see much of anything. He pulled in front of the hanger where Sammy's old pickup was parked, rain coming in through its broken passenger window, soaking the seat.

Bud opened the hanger door, going inside. Wilma Jean's new plane must be over to the side, he thought, making his way past a couple of other small planes, one that he recognized as Vern's Cessna. He felt a moment of chagrin at not having come out to see his wife's plane before this, as he wanted to be supportive, even though she'd wanted him to wait until Sammy finished the new paint job.

As Bud came around the tail of Vern's plane, Howie behind him, he could now see a trail of stuff that led right to the passenger door on what he took to be Wilma Jean's new plane—it had to be hers, for who else would paint their plane a bright pink?

Bud stopped for a moment, kind of stunned, then broke out into a big grin. He'd always felt that Wilma Jean had panache, and this proved it. The words "Cessna Cafe" were painted in bold black letters along the side of the plane.

Howie whistled. "Wow, Sheriff, this is some plane! You'd sure recognize that thing in the sky."

"From miles away," Bud grinned.

Sammy, who was leaning against the plane, asked, "What do you think of the color? I painted it all myself."

"You did a really nice job, Sammy," Bud replied. "Was it your idea to paint it pink?"

Sammy laughed. "No way. I'm more for traditional colors, but Wilma Jean thought it would stand out and make people remember it."

"I think she's right," Howie said. "But let's take a look at the damage here."

He began examining the crowbar marks on the plane's door.

"She doesn't ever lock it up," Sammy said. "But she told me she had something valuable in there this time and didn't want to take a chance, so she locked it."

Bud was surprised, wondering what kind of valuable stuff his wife would need for an air drop.

"Did she say what it was?" He asked.

"All I know is that it was something a group had asked her to drop out in the backcountry for them. Looks like that won't be happening anyway, with this rain. Maybe it was some kind of equipment."

"Hopefully something that could withstand an air drop," Bud added, now gathering up the stuff strewn across the floor, which appeared to be tents and sleeping bags and other camping gear.

Sammy said, "At least they didn't break out the window. I think we can fix up the crowbar dents and the latch, but a plane window is expensive."

The three soon had everything picked up just as Sammy's phone rang. It was Wilma Jean, who Sammy had left a message for.

Bud could hear Sammy saying, "No way! Hang on, and I'll go look."

Sammy then climbed into the passenger seat of the Cessna, rifled around a bit under the pilot's seat, then got back out.

"Wilma Jean? You still there? I looked in that little box under your seat, and the box is there, but it's empty."

There was a pause, then Sammy said, "Yes, I agree, someone had to have known it was there. That's not something you'd think of as normally being under the seat of a plane."

There was another pause, then Sammy said, "I can't believe that. Almost a thousand years? OK, I'll tell Bud. You can come out tomorrow and check everything out, but it's definitely gone. I'm going to start locking up the hanger when I'm gone. Come on out tomorrow. See you then."

Now Sammy said, "You're not going to believe this, boys. Somebody just stole the ring for a wedding Wilma Jean was going to supply tomorrow down the Green. And not just any ring, but a ring that's been in the family for almost 1000 years. Whoever it was had to have known it was under the seat."

Bud suddenly felt like a mutt. One thousand years? There was a family rumor that one of his relatives had come over on the Mayflower, but it was unsubstantiated.

"Man, my family doesn't even go back a tenth that far," Howie said.

"It has to," Sammy grinned, "Or you wouldn't be here."

"I kind of wish I weren't," Howie replied. "How in heck can I ever solve a crime like this? I need help. We've had a rail crime and now this. Bud, everything's going haywire. We may have a serial crime committer among us. I need to deputize you."

Bud replied, "Not to worry, Howie, I'll be glad to help."

They said goodbye to Sammy and headed back to Howie's, where Bud dropped him off, the rain now coming down even harder. Bud noted that it was starting to wash over the street and wondered if some of the canyons nearby weren't already flash-flooding.

He was glad to be driving back to the bungalow instead of Krider's big house. He thought about being deputized, though he knew it really didn't mean all that much, as he already helped Howie out all the time. But it would be kind of nice to be back on the force, even if just as a temporarily deputized citizen.

He now wondered if maybe he wasn't ready to get back into law enforcement permanently. Time would tell, but for now he just wanted to go home and see his wife and dry off.

9

"A ring that old would be worth some money," Bud mused.

He and Wilma Jean were having blueberry pancakes, eggs, and orange juice for breakfast, the dogs under the table, begging. It was a gloomy day outside, still pouring, and he and his wife had that rarest of things, a day off together.

Bud slipped Pierre a bite of pancake, which the little dog promptly spit out with disgust. Hoppie then tried to bury it, though there was nothing to bury it in. They both now sat staring at Bud, and he figured they were trying to telepath something to him.

"There isn't any bacon, boys, and now you're going to have to clean that up, hon," Wilma Jean advised.

"You weren't supposed to notice," Bud replied. "But did you get to actually see the ring? A thousand years old..." His voice trailed off.

"I did. It wasn't particularly beautiful or anything, no stone, just silver with what looked to be runes carved around the ring itself."

"What did they say?" Bud asked.

"I didn't ask," she replied. "I was too busy trying to figure out a good place to hide it. It was worth a fortune, and now it's gone. And I don't even have insurance yet. What I don't understand is how someone knew where it was."

"Did the person who gave it to you see where you put it?"

"Well, now that I think of it, I did tell him where I was going to hide it. I wanted to be sure someone else knew, just in case."

"Who exactly did you tell?"

"It was the bride's father."

"Then he has to have told someone else," Bud said. "How else would anyone know to steal it? And good luck selling something so unique, even the black market doesn't like things like that, as they're too easily identified."

"Unless it was going to a foreign country, Bud. Someone there might buy it. Someone in a Scandinavian country with an interest in Vikings, as that was about the ring's era, one-thousand years ago."

"An actual Viking ring or not, you'd need a certificate of authenticity, which would be hard to come by. There are so many fakes any more that even people on the black market have stopped buying stuff. It's even harder to sell things so unique."

"If people on the black market aren't buying anything anymore, how are they making money?" Wilma Jean asked.

"I don't know," Bud shrugged. "Maybe they're selling financial derivatives."

Wilma Jean shook her head, then added, "The ring did look old, but maybe there's some way of telling, like measuring the patina or something. I don't know. I just know that my air drop today is a big bust."

"Where were you going?" Bud asked, refilling both their coffee cups. He badly wanted a dollop of ice cream in his, but decided it wasn't worth the lecture about his weight, so he poured a little half-and-half in his cup instead.

"Don't worry, I'm still on my diet," he said defensively, as if Wilma Jean could read his mind.

Wilma Jean replied, "You do look like you've lost a little. I was going to supply a wedding party. They were boating down the Green and having the wedding there on the beach below Nelson's gravel pit. I was supposed to drop everything they needed to camp."

Bud now slowly sipped his coffee, wanting badly to fiddle with something. He finally started tapping his fork on the edge of his cup.

"That doesn't make sense," he said. "Are you going to pick up their supplies?"

"Not that I know of. What doesn't make sense?"

"Boaters always take their supplies with them on the boat. If they don't have room to haul the stuff in with them, how are they getting it out? Nobody abandons their gear, it's too expensive."

"They told me they're taking it out with them."

"Then why not take it in with them?"

"Bud, I have a riddle for you," Wilma Jean said. "What does it mean if you come to a fork in the road?"

Bud was puzzled and began tapping his fork even louder, thinking. Finally, he replied, "Stop and take a break for ice cream? I don't know."

"It means someone up ahead is eating with their fingers, and that's what you're going to be doing soon, if you don't stop."

Bud grinned, putting the fork down.

Wilma Jean now continued. "The father of the groom told me they needed room on the boat for the wedding party, as some are coming out and not camping, so that's why the air drop. And the ring was so valuable that he didn't want it along until they actually had the ceremony on the beach, so there would be no risk of it getting lost."

"It sounds like it's a big party," Bud said, now giving the dogs each a bite of egg.

"He said they were going down in some kind of big boat, so I would assume it's a jetboat," Wilma Jean replied.

"Well," Bud said, "Nobody's going anywhere in this storm. Have you been able to get ahold of them?"

"Not yet. They were supposed to come in from California on Amtrak, but the trains are all closed down for some reason. They can't run the river in this weather, anyway. But there's no place to stay in town, if they do make it in."

Pierre was now chewing on the toes of Bud's sheepskin slippers, apparently taking the matter of getting something to eat into his own hands, or paws, in his case. Bud tried to shake him off, but ended up bumping his knee on the table, spilling his orange juice.

"It's Pierre's fault," he said, jumping up and getting a washcloth.

"I have an idea, if I can get ahold of Krider," his wife said, ignoring Bud and Pierre's antics. "His house is totally furnished, and if I could get Kale and his wife to stay in the downstairs apartment there as sort of chaperones, maybe this wedding party could rent Krider's house until the weather's better, kind of like a B&B, though they'd have to do the breakfast part on their own."

She pulled out her phone, then stood and started walking into the living room.

"Hon," she said on her way out. "I've had this thought before, that his house would make a perfect B&B. If we could somehow get the farm, we could stand to make some cash if we could also rent his house out to tourists."

"But who's going to run a B&B?" Bud asked, wishing he had his baton. "You're way too busy as it is, and I'm not competent in those arenas, you know that. I can barely remember to scrape off my boots before coming into the house."

But it was too late, for Wilma Jean was already in the other room, talking to Professor Krider.

10

"Hon, I'm heading to the airport, then I have to go find Kale's wife to see if they'll spend the night at Krider's."

"I assume Krider is OK with the idea?" Bud asked.

"He's fine, as long as Kale's there to keep an eye on things, especially since it's a wedding party. He thinks it's a great idea for some extra income. But I need you to go over to Krider's and check everything out, make sure it's ready for company, and take your camera along. It would be a good idea to take photos throughout the house, and that way if there's any damage we can prove it."

Bud groaned. It was still raining, and he'd planned to spend some time going through his old photos. They were beginning to take over his hard drive—it seemed they proliferated when he wasn't looking, and he was going to have to take a harder line and get rid of some, though he usually ended up just going through them and reminiscing and making copies of his favorites instead of deleting things, ending up with even more.

"Are you sure the wedding party's going to want to stay there?" He asked.

"I was able to get ahold of them, and they're coming in from Salt Lake in a few hours. They flew in there and rented cars and aren't sure what to do, but they don't want to call off the wedding, in spite of the weather. It's supposed to stop raining this evening, so they're hoping they can get on the river tomorrow and I can drop off their supplies then. But I was right—they hadn't been able to find anything and were getting desperate. I quoted them a fair price and they were happy with it. I think Krider will be happy with it, too."

"Did you tell them about the ring?" Bud felt like he was interrogating a suspect.

"I did, and I got the strangest response, hon. The father of the bride just said he was sure they would get it back. Isn't that odd?"

"It is," Bud replied. "Maybe they have a family feud going on or something, where they steal each other's stuff. Come to think of it, that would make an interesting economic system, you just steal from someone when you need something, then they steal it back when they need it."

"I think there's already something like that around, hon. It's called a community exchange. People use it for bicycles and tools. There's a central location for things and you borrow and return them when done."

"Doesn't sound nearly as interesting as stealing it," Bud replied, picking up his camera as she walked out the door.

He'd go on over to Krider's and get the job done, then head for the equipment shed and spend some time changing the oil on the farm's old pickup. Maybe after puttering around for awhile he could sit under the cottonwood with the boys and think about finding a new job, assuming it stopped raining.

He'd kind of enjoyed being a slacker lately, and if he went to the farm he and the boys could hide out from everything, especially if there were more crimes afoot. Being deputized didn't mean he had to be a deputy, it was just a backup sort of thing for Howie's sense of well-being, Bud mused.

Just as he got the boys into the FJ, he got a call from a number he thought he recognized, but wasn't sure.

"Yell-ow," he answered.

"Bud? This is Maureen. Do you have a minute? Is this a good time?"

"Sure," Bud replied, wondering what was going on. It was unlike her to call him unless she was looking for Howie or Wilma Jean.

"I sure hate to take up your time," she said. "But I'm really worried about Howie, and I need your advice."

Bud's stomach began thinking about growing a knot.

She continued, "You know, Bud, I thought we had a good marriage now, though we've had some hard times in the past, but it seemed we'd worked through all that."

"I remember that, Maureen," Bud said, the knot growing. He wasn't much of one for giving relationship advice, especially to his best friend's wife.

He now asked, "Weren't you guys separated for awhile—weren't you living over in Castle Dale when Howie first started working on the force?"

"It was a hard time, Bud, and it was all my fault. I loved him from the day we met, but it took awhile for me to accept his eccentricities and learn to live with them. He's kind of a closet brainiac, and it takes awhile to realize that. He does things that one eventually understands, but it sometimes takes time."

"I understand," Bud replied. "Things that would make baton twirling look tame."

"What?"

"Oh, I was just thinking about how he has lots of eccentricities, if you want to call them that, but he's actually really smart."

"He's definitely smarter than one would think when you first meet him," she agreed. "But lately he's been going out at night a lot. He won't tell me where he's going, and when I ask, he just says I'll know soon and not to worry. But I can't help but worry. I'm worried he's having an affair or something, Bud. He only goes out at night, and I've noticed when the weather's bad he stays home. Do you have any idea where he's going? Are you guys on a case together or something? I know he was with you last night."

The knot was now almost big enough for Bud to feel. He patted his stomach, then his shirt pocket, taking out an antacid, then replied, "I wish I could say we were on a project together, but I can't. But Maureen, I know Howie well, and he's not the type to go out on you. He thinks the world of you. I'm sure it will all be explained shortly."

Maureen was silent for a moment, and Bud thought he maybe heard a bit of sobbing, but she then came back on and said, "I hope so, Bud, because I'm going to tell you something even Howie doesn't know. I'm saving it for a surprise, but I never see him anymore, except in bed snoring."

She hesitated, then added, "I'm going to tell Wilma Jean tomorrow, but I prefer to be the one to tell Howie, if he's ever home long enough. But Bud, Howie's going to be a dad. I think it's a boy. He always said he wanted a little drummer boy for the band, and now he's going to get one."

Bud was in a state of complete disbelief, but he managed to say, "Congratulations, Maureen. But can I ask how long Howie's been going out like this?"

Maureen paused, then replied, "Several months."

"And how far along is the baby?"

"The doctor said about two months."

Bud grinned. "I don't think you have anything to worry about. Howie's as good as gold. You say he only goes out at night and when the weather's good, so I suspect he has some kind of night project he's working on. He'll tell you when he's done, and until then, I wouldn't give it a second thought."

Maureen sighed, obviously relieved. "Thanks, Bud. I hope you're right—I know you're right."

"I'm definitely right," he said. "Goodnight, and again, congrats."

11

———————

Bud pulled into Krider's drive, found the hidden key in the flower pot on the deck, then opened the door into the kitchen. He stood outside for a minute before going in, wondering again how everything could be so different without things really not changing that much.

The thought of Krider's house being a B&B had never occurred to him, but that was nothing compared to the news Maureen had just whacked him over the head with.

Howie was going to be a father! Howie in that role was beyond Bud's wildest imaginings, but come to think of it, he'd noticed many times the gentle look on his friend's face when cradling Bodie or Tobie, and the cats obviously adored him, so maybe there was some paternal material there.

Maybe what was harder for Bud to imagine was being Howie's kid, but then, Howie had always shown a special affinity for kids when he'd had to deal with them, like when they would ride their bikes over Mrs. Jensen's lawn and things like that. Howie had always shown a soft touch for them, even the ones that Bud had considered more nuisance than kid, and they always responded to Howie's kindness.

Bud now stepped inside. He'd been in Krider's house a number of times to discuss farm matters, but he'd never paid much attention to the place as a potential residence or B&B. All he knew was that it was much fancier than his own tastes, though it seemed to suit the genteel professor and his even more genteel wife just fine.

He might as well get to work, Bud decided. The sooner he was done the sooner he could hide out in the equipment shed and forget everything.

He'd almost finished taking photos of the downstairs when he thought he heard a scratching sound coming from somewhere upstairs.

Normally he would think it was a raccoon or some critter who'd gotten into the house, but in light of all the recent happenings, he wished he'd brought his Ruger. He was considering going home for it, but decided he was being paranoid, and wanting to get the job over with, he went upstairs.

The scratching now sounded more like tearing and prying and was definitely coming from the master bedroom at the end of the hall. Bud quietly made his way to the door, then opening it a crack, looked inside.

He was shocked to see the redheaded guy from the Chow Down, the one called Erik. What was even more shocking was seeing that Erik was using a crowbar to pry drywall off the wall, wallpaper hanging from it in shreds.

Bud really wished he had his Ruger, but he guessed he'd have to fake it. He didn't see any sign of a weapon on the guy, so he would use chutzpah, that powerful stuff Wilma Jean always used to get through questionable times.

"Hold it right there," Bud said in his most authoritative voice.

The man was surprised and jumped several feet. Bud was ready to retreat upon the first sign of weaponry, but instead, the guy dropped the crowbar and put his hands up, saying, "I didn't do it."

"I don't know what you *didn't* do, but I can for sure see what you *did* do," Bud said. "I'm a deputy sheriff, and you're under arrest. Stand with your back against that wall, sir, and state your name. Keep your hands up."

The man looked visibly shaken and backed up to the wall, saying, "I'm Erik the Redhead."

"Erik the Redhead? That's your christened name?"

"I'm not Christian. I'm heathen, part of the remnant of the Great Heathen Army," replied Erik.

"I didn't say Christian, I said christened. But what's the Great Heathen Army?"

"My lips are sealed."

Bud groaned. "That's fine, all I need to know is your real name. Giving a false identity to a law enforcement officer is a crime, you know."

"My real name is Erik the Redhead Nelson."

"Do you have any ID?"

Erik reached into his pocket and pulled out a driver's license, handing it to Bud, who read out loud, "Carl Edward Nelson, Redding, California."

Bud paused, then said, "I thought you said your name was Erik."

"It's my..." Erik paused, then said, "Erik the Redhead's my nickname."

Bud asked, "Where did the Red part come from?"

Erik replied, "I have no idea how Redding got its name, officer. I just live there."

Bud groaned. "Never mind. Do you mind explaining what's going on here?"

"Well, it appears that I'm being detained by an LEO who wants to know how my hometown got its name. I have to admit it's an unusual situation, but it's not the first time I've found myself in such."

Bud was quiet for a moment, then said, "Mr. Nelson, Erik AKA *Carl* Nelson, my name's Bud Shumway. I'm not the sheriff here, but I was deputized by him to try to find out a thing or two about some possible criminal activity. Would you care to cooperate with me, or would you prefer to go on down to the sheriff's office and be interrogated there?"

Erik now looked nervous as he studied his feet, then said, "Criminal activity? Like what?"

"What you're doing qualifies," Bud replied. "Would you care to tell me why you're skulking around here, tearing into the walls? For all I know, you're getting ready to plant charges and blow everything up, though why you would want to do something like that is beyond me."

Erik looked surprised. "Why would I want to blow up my own house?"

Now it was Bud's turn to look surprised. "*Your* house?"

"Look, Mr. Shumway, some day I'll be able to explain this and you'll see it makes perfect sense. But for now, I'd just like to go back to my hotel and have a nice strong drink. I'll pay to get the wall fixed, but there's something hidden in there that I need. *Desperately* need."

"Like what?" Bud asked.

"I'm not at leisure to tell you," Erik replied. "But how can I find it if you're here stopping me, in my way?"

"Trespassing is illegal. Maybe you could work it out with the owner, Mr. Krider. That would be the right way to do things, wouldn't it?"

"Not necessarily," Erik muttered under his breath.

Bud was getting irritated. "Not if you're a member of the Great Heathen Army, eh? And do you sometimes wear shaggy breeches?"

"You weren't supposed to hear that," Erik said, turning red. "I was just mouthing off. I get myself in trouble all the time, just mouthing off. But what, shaggy breeches?"

"You Vikings aren't here to blow something up, are you?" Bud asked. "Would something like the world's largest steam locomotive be worthy of a Viking raid?"

Erik looked puzzled. "Steam engine? Are they still building those?"

He then pleaded, "Mr. Shumway, I need your help. I don't want anything to do with those guys, but they've got me by the short hairs —one of them will soon be an in-law and the other thinks my grandfather swindled his family, which is nonsense, but he hounds me like a hound. He keeps saying he's going to blackmail me. And please don't call me Carl, call me Erik."

Bud thought for a moment, then said, "Alright, Erik. You tell me what it is you're looking for and I'll think about things. But you're going to pay every penny to get these walls restored exactly as they were, or I'll personally throw you in jail. And if someone is black-mailing you, maybe you should get a good attorney."

Erik replied, "He's not actually blackmailing me yet. But if I tell you what I'm looking for, will you not tell anyone else?"

Bud grimaced. "I can't promise that. But I will promise to keep it in my own circle, which would be me and the sheriff," he replied.

"OK, but I'm going to be staying in this room tonight, so if it's OK with you, I'll keep looking. I'll leave tomorrow, and I'll give you however much money you think it will cost for repairs. If that's not enough, I'll leave my contact number—better still, a blank check," Erik said.

"You have a lot of nerve, I can vouch for that," Bud replied. "But you can't stay here, there are guests coming."

"I'm one of those guests," Erik replied. "My son is getting married, and they're arriving soon from California. I've been in town for a few days with the father of the bride and the guy who's threatening to blackmail me. We're getting things ready for the wedding."

Bud's head was spinning. "You hang out with someone who wants to blackmail you? Do you have a hard time finding friends? You guys were in the Chow Down the other day, right?"

"We were," Erik replied. "I saw you there with the sheriff. But can I put my hands down now? I'm getting tired."

"I didn't see your car outside," Bud commented.

"My friends dropped me off. It felt a little sketchy coming in before I was supposed to, but I needed some time to do my search. It was pretty serendipitous that the pilot for the plane who's doing our air drop had connections with this place. I was thinking I'd have to break in."

"Just how did you get in?"

"The key's in the flower pot where everyone always leaves their keys."

Bud sighed. "Mr. Nelson, what exactly are you looking for?"

He suddenly flashed back to the article he'd read about Fannie McGregor. Hadn't she sold the farm to the Nelsons? Could this be the same family?

Erik had put his hands down, and Bud thought he looked eager to get back to the crowbar.

Bud asked, "Your family used to own this, didn't they?"

Erik looked surprised, saying, "We still do, Mr. Shumway. Things back then weren't necessarily recorded like they should've been. There were no title companies to make sure things were done right. Your friend Mr. Krider had a title search done up at the courthouse in Castle Dale when he bought this, but the people there weren't very thorough. The title is clouded, and as soon as I can find the deed my grandfather told my dad was hidden in this bedroom wall, I'm going to reclaim the Nelson Farm."

Bud sighed and handed Erik a card with his phone number, then said, "Call me when you do. Until then, it belongs to Professor Krider, and you're obligated to fix the walls."

Not knowing what else to say or do, Bud turned and walked back down the stairs and headed for the equipment shed.

He knew he was remiss for not stopping Erik from vandalizing Krider's house and that he should've arrested him, but something was holding him back, something he didn't understand.

He didn't even know what to say to Wilma Jean, so he just got to work changing the oil, the boys watching as they chewed on Barkie Biscuits.

12

Howie had told Bud there was a Viking ship down on the river, but actually seeing it was another thing. They both stood on the river-bank at the state park, amazed, as several people milled around on the boat's deck while others stood watching.

The rain had finally stopped, and the boat looked less than seaworthy with several inches of rainwater on its deck, but a couple of what appeared to be employees of Green River Waterways were sweeping it off. A van with the sign *Green River Waterways* was parked at the dock, and Bud knew this had to be one of their boats.

Green River Waterways was a local boating company that supplied raft and canoe rentals and river shuttles, but Bud had never seen anything like this. He couldn't be sure from a distance, but it appeared to be a large jetboat that they'd converted to look like a Viking ship through the clever use of cardboard and crepe paper, even having a dragon's head at one end.

Howie had come by the bungalow and picked Bud up in the Land Cruiser, asking if he wanted to go on a ride-along for a few hours, since he was now a deputy.

Bud had thought it amusing after all the hours he'd spent riding in sheriff's vehicles, but decided it might be good for him to get out and about and forget all the changes coming his way. He especially wanted to forget not arresting Eric the previous day, and he wondered how much damage Erik had done to Krider's bedroom and whether or not he'd found the deed.

In his defense, he mused, part of the reason he hadn't arrested Erik was because the jail was several hours away, over in the county seat of Castle Dale, and Bud also didn't have his gun. If Erik had decided to bail on him, there was nothing he could do about it.

"This must be the party Wilma Jean's doing an air drop for today," Bud mused, watching as two more Green River Waterways vans now drove up to the dock and disgorged a party of about 20 people. They were all dressed like Vikings, and Bud could feel a high energy in the air even from where he and Howie stood watching.

"What the hay, Bud," Howie said. "Vikings! Do you suppose they're filming a movie or something?"

"If they were, we would know about it, don't you think, Howie?" Bud asked. "There are no secrets in Green River, Utah."

"We didn't know about Big Boy coming to town," Howie replied.

"That's because we don't run in railfan circles," Bud said.

"We sure as heck don't run in movie circles, either," Howie pointed out.

"Howie, I think this is a wedding party. Wilma Jean's going to drop off all their camping supplies today down on the Green. I think they're going to have the wedding on the beach and then part of them will camp for a few days as they float the river, kind of having a Viking reception as they go. I'm sure the boat company has a boatman on board to drive the thing. They'll probably go up the Colorado once they get to the Confluence and then disembark at Radium, as that's standard operating procedure.

"I bet that was one of the more interesting requests that Waterway's ever had, to create a Viking ship." Howie said. "And I bet that boatman never forgets this trip. But what's a Viking reception like? Do you suppose they'll burn the ship?"

"I think that's more of what they do for a Viking funeral," Bud replied. "I'm sure the Waterways folks wouldn't be too keen on that."

"Well," Howie replied, "I hope they have it in their rental contract. You can't be too careful when dealing with a bunch of wild pillaging Vikings."

"You sound like you've dealt with them before," Bud laughed.

"Not that I know of," Howie said.

"Actually, Howie, I have. One named Erik the Redhead."

Now that he thought of it, Bud was surprised to not see Erik in the group, which was now boarding the boat.

"A real Viking, here in Green River?" Howie asked.

"Yes, just yesterday, as a matter of fact. I'll tell you about it later."

Now a blue car drove up and parked near Bud and Howie, and they watched as a young man and woman got out, holding hands.

The man had shoulder-length red hair and looked remarkably like Erik the Redhead, and Bud guessed it must be his son. He was dressed in a hip-length white cloak and white baggy trousers, with colorful swathing bands wrapped around his legs and a large silver brooch holding the cloak in place.

The woman was perhaps the most striking person Bud had ever seen. Her long braided hair was almost white, and her skin was so fair she looked like she'd never seen the sun. Bud guessed this was the bride, Sigurd's daughter.

She wore a long trailing purple cloak over what appeared to be an ankle-length matching purple dress, and, like the groom, had a brooch holding the cloak closed, though hers had colorful beads hanging from it. The cloak had a decorative silver braid around the neck.

Now Sigurd got out of the car, followed by Erik, dressed in regular clothing. These were definitely the dads, Bud thought, as the two men walked the couple to the boat, hugged them, then returned to the car and drove away.

"That redheaded guy is the Viking I got into it with yesterday," Bud said almost in a whisper. "It doesn't look like the dads are going along on the wedding boat. I wonder why."

"Well," Howie replied. "I wouldn't want my dad on my wedding boat, would you?"

Bud laughed. He then flashed back on his conversation with Maureen, wondering if she'd told Howie the news yet.

Probably not, he figured, or Howie would've mentioned it. After all, it was big news, and it would definitely complicate things, having a baby and trying to run a drive-in and sheriff's office.

On the other hand, people had been having babies since human time began, Bud mused, and having to gather food and tend the animals and mend the tents hadn't slowed anyone down yet. He wondered how long he could keep the secret, though he knew he didn't dare be the one to tell Howie.

"Sure is a lot of change coming our way," he said, unable to help himself. If Howie did know, this would be a good cue for him to tell Bud the big baby news.

"Yup, those guys are sure in for a big change when they get that thing on the river. It's too high from all the rain for casual boating. I hope their boatman knows what he's doing."

"You don't suppose the Waterways would send a boat down if the conditions were dangerous, do you?" Bud replied. "Sometimes high water makes a river easier to run, as it covers all the rapids."

"In general, yes," Howie said. "But since this is a wedding party, you know they'll be partying and probably drinking. What do Vikings drink, anyway?"

"I don't know, mead? They probably drink whatever they can find when they're pillaging, whatever the locals have."

"They should have taken some of Old Man Green's hard cider. That would knock them for a loop."

"Or two," Bud agreed, now wondering where Sigurd and Erik had gone and why they weren't going on the boat. He now thought of Wilma Jean and wondered how soon she'd be doing her air drop. Maybe the dads were going out to prepare the camp.

"Why aren't they wearing horned helmets?" Howie asked.

"I don't think Vikings really wore helmets much," Bud replied. "Just another Viking myth."

"Do you know where they're from?"

"California, I think," Bud replied.

"Vikings in California?"

"They're everywhere, Howie. They conquered the world."

"Why did they pick the Green for their wedding?"

Bud felt the same impatience he used to feel when he was sheriff and Howie was his deputy and asked endless questions, but he patiently answered, "I don't know. Maybe because it's so mellow and they can float it for several days. Probably the nearest thing like that to California."

"Bud," Howie continued. "Hows come you know so much about Vikings?"

"I don't, Howie. I just read a little when I was trying to figure out what a Ragnarite is. Ragnar was a Viking hero."

"Oh, that makes sense now. So, you think those guys in the Chow Down were Vikings? It looks like one of them tried to pillage the railroad, or whatever you call it. Why would he do that?"

"I have no idea, Howie, but time's a wasting. Let's go on out to the airport," Bud was hoping to get out there before Wilma Jean took off.

"Sounds good," Howie replied. "But do you think they found that old ring yet? How can you have a wedding without a wedding ring?"

"I doubt if the lack of a wedding ring ever stopped a good Viking," Bud replied, watching as the boatman now untied the boat, which began drifting into the current.

"Bon voyage," Howie said.

"Good raiding and may Loki smile on you," Bud added.

"Who's Loki?" Howie asked.

"I looked it up after hearing the guys in the Chow Down saying 'By Loki.' It's the Scandinavian god of destruction. Like those little Loki missiles down in the park."

"Well, I hope Loki stays away, personally," Howie said doubtfully.

"Me, too, Howie. Maybe that wasn't the best thing to wish on their behalf."

The boat was now in the current and rapidly floating downriver as Bud and Howie got back into the Land Rover and headed for the airport.

13

"Want to go along for the air drop?" Wilma Jean asked Bud, patting the nose of her pink Cessna.

"I would love to, but I need to get back to work," Bud replied, surprised at how easily he'd managed to pack two lies into one relatively short sentence.

Howie stood looking longingly, and Bud knew he was too polite to invite himself, so he said, "Maybe Howie would like to go along."

Now remembering that Howie was about to be a father, Bud immediately regretted saying anything.

"Howie's more than welcome to come along," Wilma Jean said. "I could use a helper. I'm still new at all this."

Howie looked at Bud, then back at Wilma Jean, then at the plane, then said, "Do you think you could cover for me, Sheriff?"

Bud laughed. "Not a problem. The Vikings are all on the river, so town's probably pretty safe now."

"Vikings?" Wilma Jean looked puzzled. Bud now realized he hadn't mentioned anything to her about Erik pillaging Krider's bedroom. Maybe it would be good to go see how much damage he'd inflicted before she got back.

"The party you're supplying is having a Viking wedding on the river," Howie explained. "Did they ever find the ring?"

"Not that I know of," Wilma Jean replied. "But if you're going along, I need to reorganize a few things from the front into the back. We'll be flying back and forth a bunch across the drop site since there's so much gear. Your job will be to jettison it out the window."

Howie grinned. "Sounds like fun. I love flying. I've never jettisoned stuff out a window, but I think I could do a good job."

Bud now felt a sense of urgency. He needed to get back to Krider's in case Kale and his wife inspected things, though he was probably already too late. He still felt a sense of hesitancy about the whole thing, like he didn't want anyone to know. Maybe it was because he considered it a failure on his part to not have put an end to it.

Howie handed Bud the keys to the Land Cruiser, then set to helping Wilma Jean reorganize things. Bud was soon driving down the airport road on his way back to town.

He'd just reached the intersection with the River Road when the thought occurred to him that maybe he secretly wanted Erik to find the deed so he wouldn't be responsible for a big enterprise like Krider's farm. If Krider really didn't own it, there was no risk of them buying it.

Bud pulled over by the golf course, watching to see if a train came by, as he thought he'd heard a whistle in the distance. He wondered if the tracks were opened back up. He could see the roof of Howie and Maureen's house just down the road, and he hoped the day went by with no incidents. He knew Maureen was busy at the cafe.

As he sat there, watching a red-tailed hawk land in one of the big trees, he wondered if he was really that averse to responsibility. Would he actually prefer to see Krider lose his farm? Was he really that unsure of his abilities that owning the farm frightened him that much?

It really wouldn't be much different from what he was doing now, Bud thought, for Wilma Jean would be the one making sure the financials worked. She was good at it, and he was good at farming, so it would surely all work out.

He wasn't even sure what he wanted at this point. He watched as the red-tail preened itself, then suddenly swooped onto a lower branch, where it sat intently scanning the grass below.

Actually, he knew what he wanted, but it didn't appear to be forthcoming very soon. He wanted to be able to wander around the desert with the boys, taking photographs and enjoying life before he was too old and beat-up to do so.

As much as he loved it, farming was hard work, and there were already times he went home feeling his joints ache a little. He'd never said anything to Wilma Jean, but there had been evenings he'd had to take a couple of ibuprofen to make the pain ease off. Other times he was fine.

He felt a little guilty, now aware of why he was hoping Erik would find the deed. Of course, Krider would lose the farm, and that was a bad thing, though Bud knew Krider had done really well for himself as a professor at his local college, plus who knows what he made from his mysteries? But it would still be a bad thing for Krider to lose his investment.

Bud was a hard worker—for crying out loud, he'd been a uranium miner in his youth, he mused. But he knew he was slowing down, and as much as he loved the farm, he just didn't feel up to running the whole shebang, even with Kale as his assistant.

Sure enough, Bud could now hear a train coming as it blew its whistle at the crossing out by the old uranium mill on the other side of the river. It would soon come clattering across the old bridge and right next to where he sat.

He about jumped out of his seat when a man came up to his window, as Bud hadn't noticed anyone around. It was Billy, the rail-fan, though his mom, Dot, was nowhere to be seen.

"Howdy, officer. There's a train a' comin', can you hear it? I hope you Green Riverites appreciate where you get to live. Where I live, there ain't no trains. That would be over in Olathe, Colorado."

Bud nodded his head congenially as the train came closer.

Billy continued. "I spent a lot of time down under in Oz, and there's nothing like our great North American Trains—they not only have the greatest sounding horns, but they blow them for absolutely any reason possible. If they come across a dirt path crossing a track in the middle of a corn field with no people or cars in sight, they still blow their horns a dozen times. Love the sound of a train horn."

Just then, a freight train was on them, blowing its whistle so loud Bud had to cover his ears. Billy seemed to revel in it, and as he waved at the engineer, the man sounded the whistle again, as if to reaffirm what Billy had just said.

Finally, as the train and noise receded, Billy said, "You think town's busy now, wait a couple more days when Big Boy comes through. It took Union Pacific five years to restore just that one engine. Can you believe they originally built 25 of those monsters? The soul of America resides in that beast—it's a visual and audible work of art. And that whistle—that whistle—ohhhh, that whistle."

With that, Billy faded away back to wherever he came from, probably the green SUV in Bud's rearview mirror.

Bud shook his head. What would it be like to have that much passion for something? He kind of felt that way about his photography, but he wasn't quite as lyrical about it. Bud wondered if there was somehow a living to be made chasing trains and taking photos—that would be a nice life.

He sighed, starting up the Land Cruiser. Time to bite the bullet and go see if Krider's bedroom walls still existed.

14

Bud wondered who was sitting on Krider's porch as he pulled up in front of the farm house. Kale's car was gone, and he knew all the guests were on the Viking boat, so he thought it might be Molly, Kale's wife. Maybe she'd been cleaning and was waiting for Kale to come back and pick her up.

But as Bud got closer, he recognized the thick shock of red hair and knew it was Erik.

Bud groaned. The last person he wanted to talk to was Erik. Why hadn't he gone with the others to wherever Wilma Jean was dropping their supplies, somewhere down along the river? Surely they would need him to help set up camp.

"I made a real mess of things," Erik said glumly as Bud walked up to the porch. Bud thought he must be referring to the bedroom walls, and he frowned, not wanting to go see the damage.

"There's a handyman in town you can hire," Bud replied. "He does a good job and won't charge an arm and a leg. But you need to get on it before my wife sees it, as she's going to be a bit upset."

Erik looked surprised. "Well, I did mess the walls up, but that's not what I was referring to," he said.

Bud flipped through the contacts on his cell phone, finding the

one he was looking for, then showed Erik the number, saying, "Call him right now and see how soon he can come out. You need to get on this. My wife's wrath isn't something you want to experience, especially at close hand."

"Is she part Viking?" Erik asked, dialing the number.

Bud had to think for a minute, but as far as he knew, Wilma Jean had no Scandinavian blood.

Erik was now talking to James, the handyman Bud had mentioned, making arrangements for him to come out to Krider's and take a look at the damages. It sounded like he could come right away.

Bud sat down on the porch steps. He really should go look at the damage, but he was in avoidance mode and would wait for James. He thought about what Erik had just said.

"What else did you mess up, if you don't mind me asking?"

Erik replied, "Everything. Every dog-dang thing."

Bud waited patiently, wondering how Howie and the air drop were going.

Finally, Erik added, "My son is getting married today. I'm supposed to go out with the guys and help set up camp, but I know Bjorn's got it out for me, and I'm afraid to be around him."

"You mean the guy that was with you at the Chow Down? He did seem a little angry."

"Yes, he's very angry. He takes all this Ragnarite stuff way too seriously. But then, he's a direct descendent of Eric Bloodaxe, and that bloody Viking blood runs deep. If we'd lived a thousand years ago, Bjorn would have been a Berserker."

"What's that?" Bud asked.

"Berserkers were the craziest of the crazy in Viking war-land. They lived to kill. They literally went berserk when fighting. That's where the word came from."

"That seems a little circular," Bud replied, all of a sudden wishing he had his baton to fiddle with. "A berserker is someone who goes berserk."

"You get what I'm saying," Erik replied. "They went into trances of uncontrollable rage."

"What does that have to do with you messing everything up? Did you go berserk up there looking for the deed?" Bud hated to think of what Erik might have done to Krider's walls.

"No, and actually, I borrowed some tools from the people who live in the basement, that guy called Kale. He helped me put all the drywall back on and we even taped it all up. This handyman guy will need to fix the wallpaper and do a little touch-up painting, but it's not too bad. Look, I feel kind of bad about it...what did you say your name was?"

"Bud. Did you find the deed?"

Erik looked despondent. "No deed. That's part of what I messed up, no deed."

"Are you sure it even existed?" Bud asked.

"At this point, no. But it's been a family legend for years, the deed in the walls."

"Seems like an iffy place to keep a deed," Bud commented.

"My grandfather was a bit eccentric and didn't trust safes and banks. He had a ton of money, but he was pretty poor at keeping track of it. There's another family rumor that he hid a small fortune in the walls of that barn over there." Erik pointed at the small faded-red barn that Krider kept his lawn equipment in.

"Go in there and I'll arrest you for sure," Bud said sternly. "But your grandfather was a Nelson, right?"

Bud knew there were Nelsons in Green River, but he had no idea if they were related to Erik or not.

"Nelson, right. He had three kids, but this was before they were born, including my dad. He was a businessman and was burned out and wanted a refuge of sorts, and he had a friend who'd been through here and liked the big farms, thought it would be perfect."

Bud was beginning to identify with Erik's grandfather. A refuge was exactly what he, too, wanted at this point in his life.

"This farm is certainly that," Bud replied. "My wife and I are thinking of buying it from Mr. Krider. I'm the farm manager, in case you didn't know."

Erik looked confused. "I thought you were a deputy."

"That, too," Bud replied, not wanting to go into it all. He wanted to know more about Erik's grandfather, about his life story and whether or not he ever found the refuge he was looking for. He added, "Krider's putting the farm up for sale."

Erik replied, "Well, without that deed, it looks like I'll be bowing out of the picture."

"Where did your grandfather go after this?" Bud asked.

"California. He bought a big farm up by Redding. My mom wanted to raise horses, so that's what they did. He retired and died on the farm. I now live there with my family."

"But he sold *this* farm. Why would you think you still own it, deed or no?" Bud asked.

"It wasn't recorded right," Erik replied.

"So you want it back, even though your grandfather already got the money from it?"

"Like I said, my grandfather wasn't very good with money—well, at least not with keeping track of it, though he made plenty. Nobody's sure if he actually was even paid for the farm. For all we know, the new owners never paid him a cent."

Bud could see where things might get complicated if nobody kept track of anything.

Now, again thinking about his son, Erik sighed, "And to think my own flesh and blood is marrying into Viking royalty. Bjorn hates me for getting those kids together. His son was supposed to marry Astrid."

"Viking royalty?" Bud asked, now wondering when James would show up.

"Astrid is the daughter of Sigurd Ragnarsson, direct descendent of Halfdan Ragnarsson, Ragnar's son."

Bud was confused. "I thought nobody knows if Ragnar really existed or not."

"I personally don't think he did," Erik replied.

"Then how can she be his direct descendent?"

"I shouldn't be telling you this, Bud, but the Ragnarite Society is a secret society whose members have Viking heritage. You don't have to prove it, as that's impossible, but it's more a thing of thinking like a Viking and wanting to be one. So if someone says they're a descendent of Ragnar, in a way they're just saying they're of good Viking blood, or maybe it would be more accurate to say of good Viking fruitiness. Bjorn thinks he's a descendent of Bjorn Ironside, a real Berserker."

"Is that where the ring came from?"

Erik now looked concerned. "How do you know about the ring?"

"My wife's the one doing the air drop."

"Oh," Erik said. "It's not really missing, you know. Bjorn just stole it back."

Bud wanted to know more, but just then an old pickup drove up with the words *Diggs' Demo and Restore* on the side.

It was James, and Bud knew it would be some time before he could finish this conversation with Erik, as badly as he wanted to, for the same blue car that had dropped the bride and groom off at the boat launch had pulled up behind James. It looked to Bud like Sigurd was driving and Bjorn was in the passenger seat.

"Here's a blank check," Erik said, now nervous, taking it from his pocket and handing it to Bud. "It's signed. Use it to pay this James guy whatever it costs to fix the damage."

With that, Erik climbed into the back seat of the blue car, and they drove away.

15

Bud was in the equipment shed, under one of Krider's big tractors, trying to figure out where a certain clanging noise came from when he turned on the PTO, again wondering how the air drop was going.

He'd lined everything up at Krider's house with James Diggs, who'd promised to get started that same day, just as soon as he went and got the supplies from Ray's Hardware Store.

Bud hoped that Erik's check was good. He was kind of miffed that Erik had left and he was having to be the middle man, but he wanted it taken care of, especially since he was still Krider's manager.

Thinking back on his conversation with Erik, it seemed to Bud that, with the Ragnarite Society, one could just make up whatever one wanted and it would fly. Erik's name wasn't really Erik, and Bud now figured that everyone just took whatever name they wanted, as long as it sounded like it was Viking.

Surely Sigurd and Bjorn and Astrid weren't their real names, he thought, nor were they direct descendants of Vikings. This was America, the great melting pot, where most everyone had mixed heritage. He personally felt that it made things more interesting, but he'd actually never met anyone who claimed to have Viking ancestors.

Bud thought back to the Chow Down conversation. Hadn't Bjorn accused Erik's grandfather of some kind of nefarious dealings? Was it possible that Bjorn also thought he had some kind of claim to the farm? Was Erik's statement that Bjorn was mad about his son marrying Astrid a red herring, or was it just the tip of a confusing iceberg?

And with so many bad feelings making the rounds, Bud wondered why these guys hung out with each other. Sigurd had seemed to hint that Erik paid for everything, so was that why? And where did Erik's money come from? He didn't seem at all fazed at handing Bud a blank check. And was Sigurd the one who'd monkey-wrenched the tracks, and if so, why?

Bud now wondered where Erik's grandfather had come by the money to buy the farm in the first place, then move to California and buy another farm and raise horses. It was likely he'd used some of the money from the sale of the Green River property to buy the California one, but California would be much more expensive, plus raising horses wasn't cheap. And did Erik's grandfather have a job? How could he just go wherever he wanted like that?

Wilma Jean once told Bud he should've been an anthropologist or sociologist, the way he was interested in people, but Bud felt it was more like he was searching for some mysterious formula for how people could live their lives like they wanted and be happy.

He felt the answer was probably simply money, but he always hoped there was more to it, like determination, talent, hard work—all those things that money can't buy.

It was a hope he held close, for he knew the odds of him ever having any money were slim to none, and he really hoped to someday find real happiness. Like most everyone else on the planet, he'd probably have to work until he was pretty much ready to drop, as he knew he wouldn't have much of a retirement.

Oh well, he thought, as he discovered a broken bolt to be the source of the PTO clank. Someone smarter than him had once said it was the journey that counted, and as long as he didn't get stuck in one place and was able to keep moving, he hoped everything would work out.

He crawled back out from under the tractor and went to his workbench, looking for another bolt, then looked toward Krider's house to see if James was there, which he was.

It was then that he thought he could hear static or chatter coming from the radio in the Land Cruiser.

Shoots! Bud was chagrined. He'd forgotten all about promising to back up Howie while he was out flying. He rushed to the vehicle just in time to hear a vaguely familiar voice say, "Over."

After waiting for awhile, hoping they'd try to contact him again, he slowly walked back into the shed, deciding he should go home and get cleaned up and go down to the sheriff's office until Howie got back, just in case something was going on. He knew the office key was on the Land Rover keychain.

Back at the bungalow, Bud let the dogs into the house and gave them each a Barkie Biscuit. It had been such a nice cool day that he'd left them in the yard, where they liked to doze under the big globe willow.

He changed into clean clothes and was ready to go down to the sheriff's office when his phone rang.

"Yell-ow," he answered.

"Bud, Hum here. I've been trying to get ahold of your sheriff over there and he's not responding. Is everything OK?"

Hum was one of Bud's old buddies from when he lived in Radium, and was also the Sheriff of Radium County. Bud had worked for Hum before, and they went way back.

Bud replied, "I'm supposed to be covering for him, Hum, and I dropped the ball. I got all involved in a tractor repair and forgot to listen to the radio."

"Understandable," Hum said, knowing Bud was a good lawman and not one to normally let such things slide. He added, "We got another one of those 911 calls that bounced our way instead of yours. The incident's on your side of the river, but since I couldn't reach anyone, I sent Cal on over. Should I call him off?"

"I can't answer that until you tell me what happened, Hum," Bud replied.

"Right, right. The call came from down the Green River about eight miles. Apparently there's been an injury or possibly even a fatality, so you guys need to get the ambulance going on its way. I have the coordinates when you're ready."

"I'm ready," Bud said, pulling a pen and paper from his shirt pocket.

Hum gave Bud the coordinates, then Bud said, "Do you know any more than that? Anything that could help me get this thing going in the right direction?"

"Just that they said there might be a fatality. Some guy named Erik, and it involved a bright pink aircraft. Do you know anyone with a pink airplane? Never heard of such a thing, myself."

Bud groaned, then replied as he rushed out the door, "I do, Hum. Wilma Jean has one."

He hung up, called the ambulance, and peeled out of the drive with the Land Cruiser, gravel flying through the air.

16

Bud wondered if Erik had been the one who'd made the 911 call or was instead the one who'd been injured or even killed. Hum hadn't been clear, and it would make a world of difference in how Bud felt as he drove down the River Road, going a little too fast for conditions, but trying to be careful. He could hear the ambulance siren back behind him a ways.

Of course, he didn't want to see anything bad happen to Erik, but if Erik had made the call, that meant that Wilma Jean or Howie or both could possibly be the injured, since it had something to do with a pink airplane, which had to be his wife's. If someone else had made the call, then Erik was possibly the injured party. He wished he knew, and he felt sick thinking maybe Wilma Jean and Howie had crashed, his worst fear.

Just then, he thought he could see something in the sky coming from the direction he was going, and as he watched it come closer, he could see it was an airplane.

He stopped and got out of the Land Cruiser, looking up, and could see it was pink. There was no doubt it was Wilma Jean, especially since she'd seen him and was waggling her wings.

He couldn't recall when he'd felt so relieved, but he then started worrying about Howie, as there was no way he could know if he was in the plane with her or not. What if something had happened to him?

Bud now felt a knot tighten in his stomach. He wished he had the baton, but realized he'd left it on the back seat of his FJ, back at home. He knew there was no way he could fiddle with it while he was driving, but just holding the shiny end might help.

Just as he was starting back up, a pickup pulled up next to him. It had the words *Radium County Sheriff* on the door, and he recognized Deputy Calvin Murphy. Like Sheriff Hum, Bud knew Cal well, having worked with him back in Radium.

"Howdy, Bud. It's been awhile. Any idea what's going on?"

"There you are, Cal," Bud replied. "All I know is what Hum told me on the phone. Do you know who called it in?"

"Some guy named Erik," Cal replied. "We're sure glad you're around to take care of things, 'cause your sheriff seems to be AWOL."

Bud grimaced. "That was my fault, Cal. I'm supposed to be his backup today and I dropped the ball. Too much going on."

"Perfectly understandable," Cal replied. "You can follow me, unless you'd prefer I follow you."

"No, go ahead," Bud said as Cal pulled out. He knew Cal didn't want to eat his dust, but that was OK, as it made things easier for him to just follow along. He now thought about what Cal had said—if Erik had made the call, someone else was injured—could it be Howie?

It now occurred to him to call Wilma Jean, and he dialed her number, but he was going down between two big hills, dropping off the Mancos shale into the Morrison Formation, and he lost the signal.

Bud now followed Cal as he turned left onto the road to the Nelson gravel pit. He wondered if this Nelson was related to Erik's family. They passed the gravel pit, then the road turned and angled down, ending near the banks of the river.

In spite of not being maintained, it was a pretty good road, and Bud wasn't surprised to see the blue car that had picked Erik up parked ahead, just above the beach. He could see stuff strewn all over, and he knew that this was where Wilma Jean and Howie had made their air drop.

It wasn't too bad of a job, Bud figured, considering how many times they'd had to fly over and drop tents, camp chairs, and other camping gear. He was surprised that Wilma Jean had managed to fit it all in the plane, even though the Skyhawk was a four-seater.

Bud and Cal parked next to the car, got out, and looked around. The ambulance also arrived and parked, two EMTs getting out.

There didn't appear to be anyone around, and Bud was wondering what was going on when he heard someone call out.

"Over here!"

Not far from the air drop was a small cliff where the higher cliffs tapered out, apparently eroded away by the river. Now Bud could see someone standing beneath it, waving their hands at them, and he and Cal and the EMTs were soon on their way.

As they got near, Bud could make out two people, and one appeared to be Erik. Bud wasn't sure if the second one was Sigurd or Bjorn, but he knew it was one or the other from the blondish-white hair.

He could now make out something on the ground near their feet, something that appeared to be covered with a jacket. A foldable camp chair lay nearby, as well as a wooden box.

He could now make out legs and feet coming from under the jacket, and he knew he was looking at the body that Erik had called in. He held his breath, as the boots looked very similar to the Wellingtons that Howie wore.

He and Cal now stood over the body. Bud nodded somberly to Cal, who understood, then leaned over and carefully lifted the jacket, then placed it back.

Cal turned to Bud and said, "I don't know who this is."

Bud breathed a sigh of relief. Cal knew Howie, and Bud knew he would recognize him.

"It's Bjorn Ironside," Erik said as Sigurd nodded in agreement. Also known as Jim Watson."

"What happened?" Cal asked.

Now Sigurd replied, "He was hit in the head by that box over there."

He pointed to the wooden box near the chair, miraculously still intact though somewhat squashed and partially buried in the sand.

Erik said, "It was jettisoned out the window by whoever was in the plane."

"And it hit Jim square in the head," Sigurd added. "He was our friend, and we want justice on his behalf. It might look like a freak accident, but it was manslaughter, the result of pure carelessness. We expect you lawmen to do your job, to find out who did this and arrest them."

Bud groaned.

He knew these guys were Ragnarites, and he knew they meant business. For all he knew, they could both be Berserkers, though he didn't think Erik had the right temperament.

And he also knew the accused was his friend Howie, the Sheriff of Emery County.

17

Bud and Cal had examined the body, and the EMTs had then loaded it into the ambulance and were on their way to the hospital and coroner up in Price, since there wasn't one in Green River. Erik and Sigurd had hung back, watching.

Bud and Cal had carefully walked all around the scene, looking for anything unusual, but finding nothing.

"Looks like a pretty straightforward case, Bud," Cal said. "But I sure wouldn't want that guy's luck, I can tell you that."

Bud nodded in agreement, adding, "What are the odds? And I'm surprised that box didn't break open on impact. I wonder what's in it."

"Let's find out," Cal said, walking over to the wooden box, having first put on gloves so he wouldn't mess up any fingerprints. He opened it, pulling off gray duct tape.

He stood there for awhile, as if trying to process what he was seeing.

Bud now walked over and looked, then said, "Inuit Pies."

"Inuit Pies?" Asked Erik with a shocked tone in his voice. He and Sigurd were nearby, eavesdropping. Erik continued. "That's impossible. Inuit ice-cream bars wouldn't weigh enough to kill someone."

"Maybe they would when at drop velocity," Sigurd said. "Didn't Newton do some experiment or other along those lines?"

Erik now looked visibly shaken. "How could you possibly keep them from melting out here in this heat?"

Bud looked again in the box. It was full of the remnants of foil-wrapped Inuit Pies, chocolate-covered vanilla ice-cream bars, which had indeed melted, leaving a sticky layer on the bottom of the box among remnants of dry ice.

Cal now returned from his vehicle with his camera, and he walked around the site, taking dozens of photos.

Bud was glad Hum's deputy was there, not only to help assess the scene, but also to keep everything legal. As it was, even though Howie had supposedly deputized him, Bud technically wasn't an LEO. Besides, he needed the moral support.

They could now hear what sounded like chanting coming down the river, and Bud knew the Viking wedding party would soon arrive. Erik and Sigurd quickly left, carrying camping gear down to the beach to get ready for them.

Cal backed his pickup to where the box sat, and Bud knew he would take it to Howie's office in Green River as evidence.

"Do you think someone tossed this from the plane window to intentionally kill the guy?" Cal asked, nodding at Erik and Sigurd in the distance. "Do you know who did the air drop?"

"Wilma Jean has a new business doing just that," Bud replied. "She calls it the Cessna Cafe, and Howie was helping her. But Cal, I don't see how this could've killed the guy. It's just not heavy enough."

"Well," Cal replied, "It could have a good velocity to it by the time it hit the ground, like that Sigurd fellow said. It is wood."

The chanting had now turned into hooting and hollering, and Bud knew they needed to leave soon before the place was inundated with what he guessed were somewhat inebriated Vikings.

"Cal," Bud said, "I think we need to get out of here before we risk getting pillaged and plundered."

Cal looked mystified.

"There's a wedding party of wild Vikings coming down the river,"

Bud explained. "I'll meet you back at Howie's office. Oh, and Cal, thanks for coming."

Cal was soon on his way back up the road, but Bud lingered for a moment. For Bjorn to have been hit by the box made no sense, as the odds were just too high.

Bud now walked back to where the box had been. He looked up, wondering if it could've been pushed from the cliff above. Was the trajectory right? He wasn't sure, but it did look possible. Maybe it had been dropped from the top of the cliff. But why?

He could tell that the wedding party was now ashore, and Bud knew he really needed to go, for as soon as they found out Bjorn was dead, they'd be wanting to know more. Besides, the sun had set and the light was rapidly fading.

But instead of leaving, he now began walking in a circle around the scene, the chair in the middle, until he found tracks that he knew had to be Erik and Sigurd's, coming from the direction of their car. His and Cal's tracks soon met up with theirs, then the EMT's.

There should be more tracks, Bud thought, if Bjorn had been here. He continued searching, and sure enough, he finally found tracks that looked like they belonged to someone wearing Wellington boots. Those tracks had another set near them, and they led to an area where the tracks were intermixed, as if there'd been some kind of scuffle between the two.

Bud wasn't sure, but it now looked like something had been dragged into a nearby stand of what appeared to be poison oak, though it looked like someone had tried to brush the tracks away with some kind of broom. He stood at the edge of the stand, and he could see where the branches had been bent and broken by something being dragged. He could now see where what looked to be tracks from boots like Bjorn's emerged from the stand.

Bud paused, not wanting to miss anything.

It didn't make sense, he thought, for if there'd been a scuffle and Bjorn had been killed, why had he been the one to come out of the bushes? Or had whoever hit him thought he was dead, dragged him into the bushes to hide him, tried to brush away the scrape marks and their own tracks, but Bjorn had recovered and then been killed somewhere else later? Or did Bjorn go berserk and kill someone, dragging them into the bushes?

Now following as the boot tracks continued on, Bud could see where they headed up toward the cliff, but he then lost them in an area of sandstone. It appeared they were going to the top, but he couldn't tell for sure.

It was now almost dark, and Bud could hear another ruckus over by the camp. It was time to go. He could hopefully come back the next day, climb the cliff, and see if he could find any tracks up there.

He now grabbed the camp chair, placing it in the back of the Land Cruiser, wondering why Erik and Sigurd hadn't picked it up. Bud didn't think it was any kind of evidence, but he wanted to be thorough.

He'd barely climbed into the Cruiser when he saw a very strange sight—if he hadn't known what was going on, he would think he was hallucinating.

A group of men were coming his way, all dressed in tunics with baggy trousers and leggings, brandishing swords. He didn't know if they were just being dramatic, but he had no doubt that they were coming for him. He didn't know what Erik and Sigurd had told them, and maybe it was just good Viking fun, but he didn't want to wait to find out.

Normally a somewhat conservative driver, it was the second time in a day that he'd peeled out, sending rocks flying.

He was soon on the River Road, headed for Howie's office, happy to have escaped what he took to be the probable remnant of the Great Heathen Army, wondering when they might attack Green River.

18

It was dark by the time Bud got back to town, meeting Cal at the sheriff's office and getting the box of Inuit Pies. Cal had then gone on back to Radium, and Bud was ready to lock up when he remembered the camp chair in the back of the Land Rover.

Carefully unloading it and bringing it into the office, he tried to open it up, but it seemed to be stuck shut, so he carefully put it in the corner. He and Howie could check it out later.

Bud next called Wilma Jean, who was back home, and she'd said that Howie had gone home after they'd returned to the airport. Bud hadn't told her anything about Bjorn's death, wanting to talk to her in person.

He'd then gone to Howie's, wanting to have Howie take him to the farm to get his FJ and trade vehicles, but Howie was nowhere to be found. Bud decided to find him the next day and return the Land Cruiser then.

He thought of what Maureen had told him about Howie being gone in the evenings and wondered if she'd told him about the baby yet. Probably not, or he'd be staying home.

Could Howie really be doing some kind of project, maybe something to do with astronomy? Bud was puzzled, as he didn't think Howie would be messing around with his hobby when there was so much work to be done.

Bud had then gone on back to the bungalow, but Wilma Jean was already in bed, and he suspected she was probably exhausted from the air drop, plus having to work at the bowling alley that evening. And odds were good she'd be up early in the morning to open the cafe.

It dawned on him that he was a little like Maureen, having a missing spouse, though he generally knew where his wife was at any given time. But maybe that was why he'd been able to identify with Howie's wife so easily.

If they bought Krider's farm, he knew he'd never see Wilma Jean, what with her cafe, bowling alley, and now the flight-catering business. He wondered if she'd talked to Krider yet.

The boys had now discovered Bud was home, and he quickly gave them each a Barkie Biscuit to keep them quiet. Fixing himself some toast, Bud thought back on the sight of a group of Viking warriors coming after him, and he was glad he hadn't lived in those times.

He didn't know much about Vikings, but he did recall reading in his history class about how fierce they were, how they were pretty much quiet farmers until they went berserk and started pillaging.

He knew it wasn't really that simple, but it must've been pretty tense being in their target zone, which had apparently included most of Europe. In fact, a Viking named Cnut the Great had conquered England at one time, bringing relative peace to that country, so they hadn't been all bad.

And hadn't Leif Erikson been the first to actually discover the new world, long before Columbus ever set foot there? The ship-building prowess of the Scandinavians was primarily what was responsible for their success, allowing them to travel the world, and the fact that they trained to be warriors from babyhood helped contribute.

What would it be like to be a quiet hard-working farmer, then be called to war on some distant shore, going from a pastoral life to one of killing and plundering? They couldn't have been very queasy at the sight of blood, as names like Eric Bloodaxe would attest.

And the Great Heathen Army, a massive and violent Viking army that was supposedly led by Ragnar's sons, had struck fear into all of Ango-Saxon England, and rightfully so, for it eventually caused so much damage that the region became politically unstable.

Bud now thought of Bjorn, wondering who had killed him. It then occurred to him that Bjorn could possibly have the wedding ring somewhere on his body. He needed to contact the coroner and tell him to keep an eye out for it.

Wilma Jean had said that the bride's father was the only one who knew where the ring was, but Bud wondered if maybe she hadn't mistaken Bjorn for Sigurd, as they looked so much alike, especially with their blondish-white hair.

Bud now slipped into his Scooby Doo pajamas, then quietly lifted both dogs onto the bed next to Wilma Jean. Hoppie turned around a few times, then snuggled into his little fleece blanket at the foot of the bed, while Pierre made his way deep under the covers like a miner going for the gold, which would be Wilma Jean's warm feet.

She stirred a bit, then sighed and went back to sleep, while Bud wondered if he shouldn't get back up and lock the back patio door. He always left it open so the cool air would come in through the screen during the night, cooling everything off for the next day.

He frowned, the memory still fresh of Vikings with swords coming his way, then he turned over and snuggled down under the covers.

Bring them on, he thought, for he had a secret weapon named Pierre, though the name might throw the Vikings off, as Vikings had settled in French Normandy. Bud knew that the word *Norman* was a French word that was roughly translated as *Norse*.

But in spite of his French name, Pierre was a dachshund, a wiener dog, the fiercest dogs on the planet, bar none, and Bud figured even a bloody Viking would cower in fear at the sight.

Mess with Pierre, and they'd soon be back on their longship, hightailing it back down the Green, swords, crepe-paper dragon, and all, Bud thought.

Pierre was now yipping softly in his sleep, maybe dreaming of chasing Vikings. Bud soon drifted off, floating down the Green in a small dory full of wiener dogs, Vikings fleeing in terror before them.

19

"We're going to have some little baby peanuts," Howie said proudly as he and Bud walked along the back walkway at Howie's house.

Bud was surprised. Maureen had obviously told Howie they were going to have a baby, but had she somehow found out it was twins? And peanuts? It seemed kind of odd to call one's offspring peanuts, especially before they were even born.

Howie now pointed to a rock with the toe of his boot, then to another next to it.

"See this line of rocks?" He asked. "Each one has a peanut planted next to it. I'm watering them every day, and I think they're starting to grow, though the peanut part is underground."

Bud laughed, somewhat relieved. "Peanuts? Where in hellsbells did you get peanut plants around here, Howie?"

"I ordered them from this place on the Internet—Jimmy's Peanut Garden. I think it has something to do with the Carter family, you know, our former president. They've been in the peanut business for a long time."

"Could be," Bud replied. "But what makes you think peanuts will grow around here? I thought they needed a lot of humidity."

"Maybe, I don't know," Howie replied. "But I love peanuts, and I figured since Green River was such a perfect climate for watermelon, maybe peanuts would like it here, too. After all, they're a lot like melons, just smaller and dryer."

"Peanuts? How so?"

"Well," Howie replied thoughtfully. "They both have a kind of shell, though with a watermelon it's soggy 'cause of all the water, obviously. A peanut has good stuff inside, like a melon. Pretty simple."

Bud was incredulous. Surely Howie was kidding around. There really wasn't much of a similarity between the two as far as he could see. But who knows, he'd never heard of anyone trying to grow peanuts in Green River, and maybe Howie was on to something.

"We have two acres here, Bud, as you know, and if I can get peanuts to grow, we might have a nice little cash crop."

"No doubt," Bud replied, thinking that Howie could then also write a book about how to conjure up miracles.

Now Howie, a concerned look on his face, asked, "Do you think I need to set up some kind of misters for them? Do they really need humidity?"

"Howie, I know nothing about raising peanuts. I'm sure you'll figure it out. And once you do, you'll be the Green River Peanut Mogul. Maybe I'll start growing them out on the farm. Do you think a hundred acres would be a good start?"

Howie replied, "I don't know, Bud. Maybe I shouldn't have told you, if you're going to come right in and be that kind of competition. Two acres wouldn't be much if you're talking by the truckload."

"Yeah, it would be peanuts," Bud laughed. "But maybe you could grow some kind of specialty peanut. You could develop a new strain and call it the Green River Nut."

Howie laughed, not sure if Bud was serious or not, then said, "Green River already grows those pretty well, Sheriff."

Bud, now trying the back door on the baby thing, asked, "Has Maureen told you anything interesting lately?"

Howie looked puzzled. "No, like what?"

"Oh, nothing," Bud said. "Just wondering if town had any good rumors making the rounds."

"Well, to be honest, she may have said something, but I don't always listen to her like I should. I've been kind of distracted lately."

Bud thought of Maureen telling him how Howie was always gone at night, except when the weather was bad. He wondered if Howie was ready to spill the beans.

"Do you get enough sleep these days, Howie?" Bud asked.

"Sure, maybe not what I'd like, but adequate. But Sheriff, what's going on? Am I missing something here?"

"No, no, just checking up on you," Bud replied. "Making sure you're staying home in the evenings and getting lots of rest. You need rest when you're sheriff, as it gets stressful."

"It's not usually too bad, Sheriff," Howie said. "I guess I could stay home more, but things would be less exciting for me."

Exciting? Bud now wondered if he hadn't misled Maureen. Maybe Howie was indeed seeing someone else, though he just couldn't picture it.

"Say, Howie," Bud now changed tactics. "If you were going to have a baby, what would you name it?"

Howie now looked concerned. "It would of course depend on if it was a boy or girl, Sheriff. But can I ask you something personal? Is there something you need to tell me about you and Wilma Jean?"

Bud, now embarrassed, replied, "No, Howie, no, we're not having a baby. I was just curious, you know, wondering what the popular names were these days."

"Well, for a girl, I think there's a lot of Elizabeths and Jessicas around. And for a boy, maybe John or Mark, pretty much the old standards. Do you know someone going to have a baby?"

"Maybe," Bud replied, now eager to change the subject. "But can we go inside and have a cup of coffee?"

Bud decided it was a good time to go ahead and debrief Howie on Bjorn's death, as well as the fact that the Vikings considered him to be the prime suspect, though they didn't know who he actually was, not yet, anyway. He'd already told Wilma Jean not to tell anyone Howie was with her.

He told Howie everything he knew over a cup of coffee in their big kitchen, the cats winding in and out of Howie's legs until he finally got up and gave them some canned cat food.

"So, Sheriff, do I have this straight? I'm now a murder suspect, though nobody but you and me and your wife knows it?"

"Sounds about right," Bud replied, now scratching Bodie's ears.

"Me, the Sheriff of Emery County, a murder suspect? Are you going to throw me in jail?"

"I would, but I don't feel like driving over to Castle Dale," Bud said, again wondering if he shouldn't have arrested Erik for tearing up Krider's walls. He then added, "You'll just have to do the personal recognizance thing."

"That reminds me, Bud, I need to get the Land Cruiser back. What if somebody decides to make a citizen's arrest and I can't even make a good getaway?"

Bud knew Howie was joking, but he could tell that deep inside he was nervous.

"Howie, there's no way they could ever pin that on you. It would be impossible to prove that something you threw from a plane hit someone on the head. And even if it did, it would be an accident."

"What if they had an eyewitness?" Howie asked. "Did the two guys mention if they actually saw it?"

"No," Bud replied. "But we didn't ask them. I figured we'd be in contact with them later for more questions."

"What did they say it was that hit him on the head? A tent?"

"No, Howie, it wasn't a tent. And even if they somehow managed to get you into a courtroom, the evidence wouldn't hold up."

"Get me into a courtroom? That would mean an arrest, Sheriff. Seriously, are you going to arrest me?"

Bud had the feeling Howie wasn't really even listening to him.

Howie continued, "Man, who's going to take care of my little peanuts if I'm in prison? And I need to start painting the drive-in so we can open it back up."

"Howie, you're not going to prison. But who's going to run the drive-in?"

"I haven't figured that out yet," Howie replied. "But Bud, what exactly was it that hit the guy in the head and killed him?"

"You won't believe this, Howie, but it was a box of Inuit Pies. They're sitting by your desk at the office."

"Inuit Pies? Man, Sheriff, you know they'll be a melted mess by now."

"They were already melted," Bud replied. "Let's go get my FJ, and then we can go check them out."

"I really don't think I can take a lot more," Howie moaned, putting on his jacket as Tobie batted at the arms. "I haven't been able to practice with the band for weeks, Bud. I really need some time off, and things just keep getting more hectic."

"And they're gonna get even more so in about eight or nine months," Bud said to himself as they walked out the door.

20

It was evening, and Bud sat on the front porch in the cool air, the dogs at his feet, watching his wife water her petunias during a rare moment when she was home. Bud knew she would soon be leaving for the bowling alley.

"I can do that for you," he offered.

Wilma Jean replied, "Thanks, but this is my therapy, one of the few times I can relax. But hon, do you have any idea why there would be gravel in my flowers? I mean, they're clear up here on the porch—come to think of it, there's gravel scattered all over."

Bud grimaced. He should have noticed and cleaned it up before she got home.

"I reverted to my younger and wilder days for a moment," he replied. "I'll take care of it."

"You mean you spun out in the drive and threw all this up here?" Wilma Jean sounded irritated.

"In my defense, I'd just got a call from Hum and was worried about you and Howie," Bud said.

"Oh," she replied. "Well, maybe you should pull in forwards from now on."

Bud had gotten in the habit when he was sheriff of parking with his rig facing out so he could make a quick getaway in case something happened.

"Just one last reminder of my old life disappearing," he said.

"Your old life? Are you missing being sheriff?"

"I don't know. Not really, but the thought of running Krider's farm has me kind of intimidated," Bud replied.

"Hon, you already run Krider's farm," Wilma Jean reminded him.

"I guess it's psychological," he said.

"Yes, it's all in your head. Krider and I had a nice talk yesterday. I didn't get a chance to tell you, but it looks like we may be close to coming to an agreement. I'll sit down with you when I get home and go over it."

Bud was surprised. For some reason, he'd gotten used to having the matter in limbo and had even hoped it would stay that way.

"Are you sure he really owns the farm?" Bud asked.

"That's an odd thing to ask," Wilma Jean replied. "Why would you ask that?"

Bud told her about how Erik had been looking for the deed, swearing the farm was his.

"That explains why I've seen James over there for the past day or two," she said.

"He should be done by now," Bud noted. "Come to think of it, I should run over there and see if he's still around and pay him."

Bud now wondered what he'd done with Erik's blank check. He asked, "Is my blue-plaid shirt in the wash by any chance?"

"It is if you haven't washed it," she said.

Bud went into the laundry room, pulling the shirt from the laundry basket. He was relieved to find the check still in his pocket. He would go see James right away before he actually did lose the check.

He loaded the boys in his FJ and headed for the farm. It would be a good idea to check and see how James had done, though he had a good reputation for doing quality work.

Pulling up in front of Krider's house, Bud saw that James' truck was still there, so he went on inside.

"I'm just cleaning up," James said. "I should be out of here in about 15 minutes."

"You did a really nice job," Bud said, relieved. "How much do we owe you?"

"Let's see," James stopped for a moment, adding up the hours in his head, then said, "$350. That includes materials."

"That seems fair enough," Bud replied, now filling out Erik's check. "Just make this out to James Diggs?"

"That's fine."

Bud hadn't looked at the check before, but he now read, *Carl Nelson, President, Inuit Pie Co., 1221 Inuit Pie Way, Redding, CA 96001.*

He stopped and read it again. Inuit Pie? President? Bud was mystified. Apparently he'd missed something, because it looked like Erik the Redhead was not only a Viking, but was also the president of the very same company that had made the product that Howie had supposedly jettisoned from the plane, whacking Bjorn on the head and killing him.

Did Erik somehow have something to do with Bjorn's death? The antagonism between the two was high, Bud thought, recalling the conversation at the Chow Down, but it seemed Bjorn had more of a chip on his shoulder than Erik did, possibly over some supposedly dishonest dealings with Erik's grandfather.

Was it somehow related to the Inuit Pie Company? Bud still couldn't figure out why Bjorn would hang out with Erik if he resented him so much. But if Erik was president of a company as successful as Inuit Pie, he would have plenty of money, and Sigurd had almost come out and said that was why Bjorn came along.

James had now left, and Bud decided he needed to go into town and pay a visit to the Melon Harvest Grocery and Deli before they closed for the day. He wanted to pick up a few things, and the boys were almost out of Barkie Biscuits.

But as he was almost to the grocery store, he saw a green VW Bug go zipping by. He at first thought it was Maureen, but he soon decided it must be Howie, as Maureen was a conscientious driver and never drifted through stop signs.

On a whim, Bud decided to follow the VW. He knew he'd have to stay back a ways to not be noticed, but he might be able to figure out where Howie was going every evening and thereby reassure Maureen.

They were soon on Long Street, heading toward the Bookcliffs, and as they came to King's Lane, where Bud and Wilma Jean's bungalow was, the dogs started wagging their tails, thinking they were going home.

"We're not going home yet, boys," Bud said. "We're on a low-speed chase, kind of like the way you guys go after rabbits—slow and lazy."

They were soon past King's Lane, and the dogs now settled back down. Bud was soon near the big dome house where Wilma Jean's friend Carolyn had a small horse set-up, giving riding lessons and boarding horses for people passing through. He could see her out weeding her garden and was going to wave, but she didn't look up as he went by.

It had been easy following Howie so far, but now the road got more curvy, and Bud wasn't sure when Howie might turn off, so he had to stay a little closer to the VW. Bud didn't want to lose him, plus the sun was setting and it was getting harder to see.

Several miles later they finally reached the end of the road, where Howie went through an open gate with a no trespassing sign, and Bud knew they were on the Rose Ranch where Long Street ended. It had always amused Bud that the farm road was still called a street way out here, miles from town.

Bud hesitated, almost stopping. He didn't feel comfortable entering the ranch property, especially since it was signed no trespassing, but he did know that many ranchers put up such signs more for liability issues than to actually keep people out.

He decided to keep going, now following the VW's taillights, as it was almost dark. The little car soon pulled up in front of the main ranch house, an adobe style with a second story. Howie got out and went inside without even knocking, and Bud could see he was still in uniform.

Bud knew Cassie Rose, the ranch owner, as she was a high-school science teacher. Her husband had died a few years ago in an accident, and she hadn't remarried, leasing the ranch out. She was very attractive, about the same age as Howie, and considered to be quite the catch, but she'd apparently never met anyone she wanted to let catch her, as she was still single.

Bud sat and waited, feeling guilty for spying on his friend. Before long, he saw the downstairs lights go off and the ones upstairs come on, and he now thought he could make out someone in the upstairs window.

Suddenly, the lights went out, the entire house now dark. He waited for awhile, but no lights came back on and no one came out.

Bud decided he'd better leave while he could still see the road, as he didn't want to turn on his headlights, knowing they might notice him.

Once back away from the house at the gate, he turned his lights back on. Slowly driving into town, he thought again about Cassie Rose. He could see her and Howie being good friends, since they both loved science, but was there something else going on? Could he have been wrong when he told Maureen not to worry?

Bud headed back to the bungalow on King's Lane, feeling lost and desultory at the thought that he really didn't know his best friend as well as he'd thought, maybe not at all.

21

Bud sat on the front porch, absent-mindedly twirling the baton as the dogs ducked, trying not to get hit, having given up long ago on catching it. It was almost noon, and he was trying to think of something that would be good for lunch, but since he hadn't made it to the store the previous evening, his choices were limited.

His phone rang, and he could tell from the caller ID it was Howie.

"Yell-ow," Bud answered.

"Sheriff, Howie here. Are you home?"

"I am," Bud answered, wondering if Howie was planning on stopping by.

"Sheriff," Howie continued, sounding somewhat excited. "Do I have some news for you!"

"What's up, Howie?" Bud asked patiently, continuing to twirl the baton, thinking maybe Maureen had finally told Howie about the baby.

"Well, last night, after I did my usual stuff, well, you know, then I stopped by this guy's house for a little bit."

Bud wondered exactly what Howie meant by doing his usual stuff but didn't ask, thinking about his visit to the Rose place.

Howie continued, "His name's Jimmy, and he lives over on

Solomon Street. Somebody told me this Jimmy guy was a real whiz at Garage Band."

Bud wasn't sure what Garage Band was, but he figured it might have something to do with music from the sound of it. He didn't want to interrupt Howie, as it was a rare thing for him to be on a roll like this—maybe even a thing of wonder, Bud mused.

Howie continued. "So, I stopped by, and we went into this guy's basement rec room and he fired up his computer and started showing me what he could do. He was making up a song and doing the background for it automatically and all kinds of other sounds, and he had a guitar, so I started playing along, and before you knew it, we were having a regular band session, but without having a band. I was pretty excited, I can tell you that!"

Howie paused to catch his breath, then added, "Man, I'm telling you we were really rocking, Sheriff, when all of a sudden we could hear some guy coming down the stairs yelling at the top of his lungs. Well, this big guy opens the rec room door, yelling something about 'Shut it down! Shut it down! You're playing way too loud.' But when this guy sees me sitting there, he gets real quiet. See, I was still in uniform, Bud. You still there?"

Bud assured Howie he was indeed still listening.

Howie said, "So this fellow, who I took to be Jimmy's dad since Jimmy's still in high school, he starts telling me what a good boy Jimmy is and talks about all the good things he does, about how he rescued this mama cat with her kittens one time, and he's just going on and on until Jimmy finally says, 'Dad, he's not here to arrest me, we're just playing music.'"

Howie paused, laughing, then continued. "His dad looked really embarrassed, but then he told Jimmy that he used to play drums in high school. I guess Jimmy never knew this before, so the dad, he takes over the drum part on the computer from Jimmy and man, he sure did have the magic touch. Before long we were playing even better and louder and Jimmy was doing the controls and before we knew it we had ourselves a tune all recorded and mastered on this Garage Band and everything."

"But Howie," Bud asked. "Does this mean you're disbanding Howie and the Ramblin' Road Rangers for a new digital electronic sound? Do you think that's a good idea? How about Maureen and Barry?"

"Oh, no, Bud, not at all, It's the opposite, actually. We're now going to have a drummer and a sound mixer. We'll still have Maureen on honky-tonk piano and Barry on stand-up bass."

"That's good," Bud replied.

Howie continued. "But we're really coming up in status here, Sheriff. Jimmy's dad, Harold, is president of the cemetery board. We now have a pretty illustrious group going—the president of the cemetery board, Maureen as the manager of the Melon Rind, and Barry as the head mechanic down there at the state highway shop, and me as the county sheriff. If we get any more brass behind our names, we're going to have to shut it down because lightning will strike us all."

Bud laughed, then asked, "So Maureen's going to keep playing for the band?"

Howie sounded puzzled. "Of course she will. Why wouldn't she? It wouldn't be the same without her."

"Just like it wouldn't be the same if she weren't in your life, right?" Bud asked.

"Bud, why would you ask something like that? Did Maureen tell you something I should know?"

Bud could see things were going south fast, so he tried an old irrigation technique—the diversion. "Howie, I just want to be sure everyone around here appreciates everyone else. You know, with rampaging Vikings around, who knows what could happen? The remnant of the Great Heathen Army could strike at any time."

"Are those guys still around, Bud? I haven't heard a word about them since they went down the river. Are they looking for me?"

Bud now felt bad, replacing his friend's happiness with worries about prison.

"Howie, I think they're long gone, and I can't tell you how happy I am to know you and Maureen will keep the band going, no matter what."

"No matter what? Is something coming that I should know about? You're sure sounding all cryptic and mysterious lately, Bud."

"No, no, I mean even when you find fame and fortune."

"Well, if we find fame and fortune, I can tell you for sure we'll keep the band going. But anyway, Sheriff, I need to git. I gotta oversee all the oncoming chaos at the park."

"Chaos?"

"That big steam engine's coming in tomorrow, and they're having something called Big Boy Daze. I need to make sure all the vendors and everyone paid their fees and don't get into any fights over who sets up where. Being sheriff isn't always easy, as you well know."

"I know, Howie, I know," Bud replied. "*Not* being sheriff isn't that easy sometimes, either."

"Well, they asked us to play at the park this evening. We haven't been practicing at all, but I wrote a song for it. But now I'm wondering if I shouldn't be laying low."

"Howie," Bud replied. "I don't think you need to worry about anything."

"Well," Howie said. "I'd sure appreciate it if you'd come to the concert, Bud, just in case."

Bud sighed. He really would prefer to just stay home with the boys, maybe look through his photos or something. The idea of being around a crowd wasn't his cup of tea.

Finally, he said, "I'll be there, Howie, but really, there's no need to worry."

He hung up, wondering what the evening would bring, slowly twirling the baton.

22

It was one of those perfect autumn days when Bud just wanted to go drive around the Big Empty, enjoying the golden tamarisk and rabbit-brush along the big wide sandy washes that ran only after a big rain, reveling in a world of gold and blue and white—golden plants, deep blue sky, and white Mancos clays.

Bud was right where he wanted to be—in his beloved desert. Unfortunately, he wasn't out taking photos, but was instead on his way along the River Road to the site of Bjorn's accident, or murder, depending on how things shook out.

Things were different when one had a destination, he thought, as opposed to wandering around with the dogs taking photos and looking for old historic junk, like the old wrecked bullet-riddled car he'd just passed which had been rusting away in the desert since he'd been a kid.

It was more fun just wandering, and there was really nothing to keep him from doing so other than his need to try to figure out what exactly had happened that day when Howie supposedly jettisoned a box of Inuit Pies onto Bjorn's head.

Bud knew it was unlikely for Howie to throw the box from the plane and hit Bjorn, and he wanted to know what exactly had transpired that day of the Viking wedding. No one in the wedding party was there, as they were on the river, so that left Erik and Sigurd as suspects.

Sigurd had been adamant about justice and finding out who'd thrown the box from the plane, but nobody had heard anything from him since, so Bud wondered if he wasn't protesting too much. Maybe he'd somehow engineered it all, but Bud had no idea why Sigurd would want Bjorn dead.

It seemed like Bjorn wanted the others dead, not vice versa. Bjorn was mad at Erik over something Erik's grandfather had supposedly done, and he was also mad at Sigurd because Sigurd's daughter, Astrid, had chosen Erik's son, Arne, over Bjorn's son. Bud had no idea what kind of drama all that had involved, but it left him with the impression that Bjorn was the one with issues, not the other two.

Had the others killed Bjorn because they were tired of his incessant negativity and accusations? That didn't make sense to Bud, for he knew a lot of people were difficult to be around, and they didn't typically get killed.

Now reaching the site of Wilma Jean's air drop, Bud parked the FJ and began carefully circling the area, looking for anything that could be a clue. Erik and Sigurd's tracks were still there, though less distinct, and he and Cal's tracks were also visible, as well as those of the EMTs.

Bud again tracked Bjorn's Wellington boots up onto the rocks, but since the light was now better, he noticed they continued on through a sandy area, then on up the hill behind the cliffs.

Following the tracks as he huffed and puffed, Bud was soon on top. He could see for miles, the San Rafael Reef to the west, the Henry Mountains to the south, and the Bookcliffs to the north. To his immediate east he could now see down on the Green River, where he saw what looked like two yellow rafts lazily floating along.

He loved being up high like this, and he never could understand why he didn't like flying. All he could figure was that he liked having solid ground beneath his feet. Maybe if he'd grown up to be a seafarer, like a Viking, he wouldn't mind the instability of being in an airplane, but he knew he would never feel otherwise.

Now he turned to the southeast, where he thought he saw something out of place. He couldn't see the river that far distant, but he thought he could make out something shimmering just above where the river ran. It seemed odd, but the more he studied it, the more he realized he was looking at dispersed smoke, the kind you see where an entire area might be on fire, as opposed to a single plume.

He wondered if Ruby Ranch might be burning their ditches, but after studying the landscape, he decided the smoke was too far south. It really did look as if the banks of the Green were on fire, and he knew this time of year a lot of the bushes and grasses would have dried up, making good fuel, in spite of the recent rain.

He watched as the smoke became more distinct, and he knew the fire was now growing. Pulling his cell phone from his pocket, he dialed the Radium County Sheriff's Office.

"Radium County Sheriff, Cal Murphy speaking."

"Say, Cal, Bud Shumway here. I'm watching what looks like a fire over in your part of the country. You might want to contact the BLM and see if they know anything about it."

"Could it be over on Ruby Ranch?" Cal asked.

Bud replied, "No, it's probably a good six or eight miles on down from there."

"On the river?"

"Looks that way," Bud said.

"We had some mountain bikers start one over here on Potato Bottom recently," Cal said. "I'll contact the BLM wildland fire crew, Bud. Thanks for letting us know."

"You bet," Bud replied, watching as the smoke got even thicker. "It's bad news for any rafters down there."

"It sure is," Cal replied. "If it's bad enough, they'll probably get a chopper out to get them off."

"I just saw a couple of rafts going downriver. But say, Cal, did you ever have any idea about what could've happened with the guy supposedly whacked on the head by the box? Did your photos show anything?"

"You mean the air-drop victim?" Cal continued, "I talked to Hum about it, but none of us really have any clues. I have those photos if you want them, but they didn't turn up anything."

"Well, thanks anyway, Cal," Bud replied. "Give me a call if you're ever in the area."

"Roger, and 10-4," Cal replied, hanging up.

Bud recalled working with Hum down in Radium one winter, and it had been nice working with a smoothly run team. He'd learned a lot, and he missed his friend for a moment, but as he turned back to the action down on the river, he was glad he was back in Green River country.

23

Bud watched from the distance as what had been gray tendrils of smoke now became black clouds, and he knew for sure the river bottoms were on fire. He knew it had to be human-started, as there were no clouds in the sky for it to be from lightning.

He now turned his attention back to the boot tracks, noting where they'd gone right to the edge of the cliff, much closer than he would've dared trust his own balance. Now the tracks seemed to pace back and forth along the cliff's edge.

Bud stepped back, a bit of vertigo setting in. He was afraid of heights, part of why he didn't like flying, and standing on the edge of the cliff was too heady, like he would just slip over the edge, like a box of melting Inuit Pies.

It appeared that someone had stood on the cliff and waited for Bjorn to step exactly where they'd thought the box would land, then pushed it off, conking him square on the head and killing him. Yet the tracks were Bjorn's! It was all very confusing, Bud thought.

He felt like he imagined Leif Erikson had felt when he discovered America—it was an exciting discovery, but what was he supposed to do next? Of course, Leif was looking for new land to colonize, but there was no evidence he'd returned after his discovery. Like Leif had abandoned settling in America, Bud thought he might have to likewise eventually abandon his newfound theory.

It just didn't make sense to stand on top of a cliff and wait for your victim to walk exactly where you wanted so you could sneakily dispatch him from above. And how could Bjorn drop a box on his own head, and would it even be something a Viking would do if they could?

Didn't Vikings revel in one-on-one warfare with swords and axes and such? Wouldn't sneaking around dropping boxes on the enemy's head be considered dishonorable?

Bud wasn't sure what kind of protocol Vikings had for their battles, but he wondered how often they had cliffs to drop things from. Surely air drops weren't a standard part of their playbook.

He again watched the fire down on the river, which was steadily growing. He thought he could now see a distant helicopter, but it soon vanished in the smoke. He remembered what Howie had said about Vikings burning their ships, but surely the wedding party was long off the river by now.

It was getting on toward late afternoon, and he wanted to go home and spend some time with the dogs before pretty much wasting his evening at the Big Boy extravaganza.

But in spite of wanting to get back home, Bud sat on a big rock, watching a dozen or more buzzards wheel though the sky, high above. He knew they were on their annual southern migration from points north, and he kind of wished he could go with them.

Green River didn't have the harsh winters they had in places like Montana, but it would still be nice to go on down to southern Utah, where the early Mormons had wintered over. They'd even grown cotton there, near the town of Santa Clara.

This reminded Bud of Howie's peanuts, and he wondered if you really could grow them here. It was getting late in the season, and hopefully they would bear nuts soon.

He next wondered when Maureen would tell Howie about the baby, and his thoughts then turned to Krider and his farm, wondering what Krider and Wilma Jean were planning.

As the sun moved lower in its journey through the sky, Bud felt sleepier and sleepier. His back against a large rock, he was soon asleep, his head nodding against his chest, the scent of rabbitbrush in bloom flooding his senses as he slept like a baby, unaware that below him crawled a large rattlesnake, its senses filled with something it couldn't quite identify, but something it knew must be a danger.

As Bud twitched in his sleep, now dreaming of the baton, the snake struck, its fangs catching for a moment in Bud's khaki pants. It then coiled back and away, ripping the material in two matching strips, slithering away into the rocks.

Bud suddenly woke, wondering what had awakened him and how long he'd been asleep. He stood, gazed over to the smoke, noting the fire was still growing, then hiked back down the hill, making his way around the rock outcropping and finally to his FJ.

As he got in, he reached down to scratch his leg, which stung like he'd gotten into poison oak. As he touched his leg, he noted two long scratches, as well as the tears in his pant leg.

He immediately knew he'd been close to getting snakebit, and the animal had actually released some venom, which many times snakes won't do in what's called a dry bite, as most snakes preferred to save their venom until they were sure they had something edible at hand.

All that had kept the snake from injecting the venom into Bud's leg had been his thick cotton pants. The snake had instead managed to scratch Bud's leg with the tips of its fangs, releasing enough venom to irritate the skin.

Bud immediately washed the scratches with a jug of water from the FJ, then headed back to town, wondering if he shouldn't go to the clinic just to be sure he wasn't really injured.

He'd spent his whole life in the desert and had rarely seen a snake, yet alone been bitten by one. And it was odd it had happened when he was asleep, as snakes aren't usually aggressive and strike only when messed with.

His leg was getting itchier, so he decided he should at least have Dr. Rocky check it out. Stepping on the gas, he left a rooster tail of dust behind him as he wondered if snakes could give you rabies.

As he pulled into the clinic's parking lot, he wondered what the doctor would do, and if this would keep him from going to the Big Boy event like he'd promised Howie.

In a way, he'd rather be snakebit than deal with crowds, but he figured it would be his luck to end up having to deal with both.

24

Bud opened the clinic door, told the woman at the desk what had happened, then sat down to wait.

He couldn't believe his eyes to find he was sitting across from Erik, who was twitching and generally looking miserable.

"You OK?" Bud asked with concern.

"Not really," Erik replied. "I had no idea there was poison ivy along the river."

"That's miserable stuff," Bud commiserated. "But it's probably poison oak."

"And you?" Erik asked. "You OK?"

"Nothing bad, just snakebite."

Erik looked shocked. "You mean like a rattlesnake?"

"Exactly," Bud replied, pointing to his torn pant leg.

"Shouldn't you be in the ER?" Erik asked.

"The nearest one's an hour away," Bud replied. "I'll be OK."

Just then, the nurse called Erik's name.

"I think you should go ahead of me," he told Bud.

"No, you go on in. They'll get to me eventually," Bud replied, picking up a copy of *People* magazine.

Erik looked doubtful, but followed the nurse into the back, trying not to scratch himself.

He wasn't gone long, now carrying a large tube of what Bud figured to be an anti-itching creme.

"Did they fix you up that fast?" Bud asked.

"It's definitely poison oak. They gave me a shot of something, maybe cortisone. I feel better already."

A woman and small child had come in while Erik was in the back. The nurse now called Bud's name, but he motioned for the woman to go on back.

Erik said, "Really, should you be waiting like this? If the venom gets to your brain..."

"That's the Mojave rattler, down in Arizona," Bud replied. "The ones here just go to your heart and cause a heart attack. But say, Erik, since you're here, would you mind if I asked you a couple of questions?"

Erik looked around to see if anyone might be listening, then sat down next to Bud, eyeing the torn pant leg.

Bud continued, "First of all, how did the wedding go?"

Erik smiled. "I heard it went great, well, at least until they arrived at camp and found out about Bjorn. Sigurd and I set up camp there for them near where Bjorn was killed, then we went back to the Prickly Pear. We're both super sensitive to bugs and stuff, so we don't camp."

"And poison oak," Bud added.

"I'm not sure where I got this, maybe over by the golf course," Erik said. "I went for a walk by the river after the funeral."

"Funeral?"

"They had Bjorn's funeral today. They sent his ashes on a small boat down the river. It was sad."

Bud paused, then said, "I'm sure it was. Is his son here?"

"Yes, he's around somewhere, probably with the others."

"Well, I hope you're all fixed up with the poison oak thing. But did you and Sigurd actually see what hit Bjorn? I mean, did you see it fall from the sky?"

Bud knew they'd told him they had, but he was wanting to hear the story again to see if it had changed any.

"We didn't see it, no," Erik answered, distracted and trying hard not to scratch. "Sigurd told me to say we did, but we didn't. No idea why he wanted that. We were over gathering the air drop stuff and taking it down to the beach by the river. I didn't even know there was a chair over there until I saw something and figured the air drop had missed. When we went over to see what it was, we found Bjorn and the box. I dialed 911. He already looked like he was dead and wasn't breathing. I'd just as soon forget it." He now started scratching again.

"When you get back to the hotel, try soaking in a tub with baking powder in it," Bud advised. "It neutralizes the oils in the plant that make you itch. Do you think Sigurd had anything against Bjorn?"

Erik now looked around again. "Not that I know of, except getting tired of him grousing around and also having to take care of his family."

"Did you have anything against him?"

"I feel like I'm in court again," Erik sighed. "But no, we put up with him because he was Sigurd's half-brother."

Bud now paused, then asked, "Erik, do you know anyone who would want to blackmail you?"

"You mean with a box of Inuit Pies?" Erik asked. "No, not really, except maybe Bjorn. But I don't know if he was capable of it or not."

"You don't think he would do it?"

"I'm not sure he actually had the ability to do something like blackmail. He had a business for awhile, but he drank everything away. He was always trying to control other people. Even his own son disowned him over the wedding thing. The kid had no interest in marrying Astrid, but Bjorn thought he should."

"Why?"

"It had to do with Viking royalty. He had it in his mind that she was royalty and his son would somehow become rich and famous if he married her."

"Is Astrid rich and famous?" Bud asked.

Erik laughed. "Hardly. She's a college student. Her dad, Sigurd, is a Harley-Davidson mechanic. Her mom works in a retail store. But aren't you getting close to passing out or something?"

Bud laughed. "No, I'm fine. But where are all the Vikings?"

"They're still around. They were able to get spots at the state park, so they're all camping, but there might be a resort rental opening up soon, not sure where. We're all wanting to see this big steam engine everyone's talking about. But I need to go. I'm starting to feel tired, maybe from the shot."

"Go get some rest," Bud advised. "But one last question. Do you think the sheriff here is in any danger?"

Erik looked surprised. "Danger? How would I know? I hardly even know the guy."

Just then, the nurse showed the woman and child out and called Bud's name.

"Well, I hope you all enjoy your time here in town," Bud replied. "And as far as Bjorn goes, I really want to figure out what happened."

Erik's brow furrowed and he said, "Good luck, but you're not going to figure anything out if you die. You're probably on your last legs—or leg—right now. I don't understand why you're not more worried about being bit by a rattlesnake. But I will say this, you're a tougher man than any Viking I've ever met."

As the nurse showed Bud into the back room, he smiled at Erik's concern, then wondered what he'd meant when he said he felt like he was in the courtroom again.

In Bud's experience, most people had never been in a courtroom, but it appeared that Erik had been there at least once, and he wondered if it had anything to do with the bad dealings between Bjorn and Erik's grandfather.

Unfortunately, Bjorn was no longer around for Bud to ask, but he did have a son, and if Bud could find him, maybe he could answer a few questions.

"You're good to go," Doc Rocky told Bud after cleaning the two scratch marks. "But if you're going to hang out with the rattlers, I would recommend getting some good snake boots. You're a pretty lucky guy."

With that, the nurse handed Bud a tube of something that looked exactly like the stuff they'd given Eric, and showed him the door.

25

It was getting late, and Bud decided to swing by the park and see when Howie and the Ramblin' Road Rangers would play. He really didn't want to go, but he'd promised Howie, and he hoped to have time to go home and check on the boys first.

Leaving the medical clinic, Bud watched a long sleek silver Amtrak train stop at the old art-deco station. He couldn't believe his eyes as it disgorged a long line of people, Bud wondering where they were all going to stay. He knew they were here to see Big Boy.

The park was packed with vendors, tents of every size and color selling everything imaginable, most of it having nothing to do with trains. A big banner hung from the Athena missile, reading, "Welcome, Big Boy Railfans!" People milled everywhere, talking, eating hot dogs and slices of watermelon, and strolling from tent to tent. It reminded Bud a lot of Melon Days, but with lots more people.

Bud walked to where the stage was, and sure enough, he found Howie and the band setting up. He saw no sign of Jimmy or his dad.

He noticed the same train man he'd talked to out by the golf course, now sitting at a nearby picnic table. Wondering if he'd had any luck finding who'd pulled the rail, he walked over to talk to him.

"Howdy," he said. "I don't know if you remember me, but I'm Deputy Bud Shumway."

Bud assumed he was still a deputy, since Howie hadn't un-deputized him. In any case, he figured it would give him a leg up on learning anything confidential.

He continued, "I was there with the sheriff investigating that sprung rail over by the golf course. I was wondering if you'd had any luck finding out who did it."

The man shook his head, saying, "No luck at all. Just not enough clues, and nobody knew nothing."

Bud thought back to Billy's mom, Dot, and wondered if the man had bothered to talk to her, but he said nothing. Feeling a little uncomfortable, he started making small talk.

"Quite the event here, eh? When's the train coming through?"

"It should arrive tomorrow morning around 10. I'm on security. We have a number of guys to keep people from getting too close, as it's dangerous and people get overly enthused—not to mention soaked when the steam lets off."

"I could see that happening," Bud replied, now wanting to go see Howie.

The train man continued. "Green River's been designated a Big Boy stopover. The train will sit here for an entire day and night, letting people take photos, meet the engineer and conductor, that kind of thing."

Bud was surprised. "Do you think that's a good idea?"

The train man looked puzzled. "Why wouldn't it be?"

"Aren't you worried about a Viking raid?"

As soon as the words were out of his mouth, Bud realized how ridiculous they sounded and wished he could take them back.

The train man looked at him, a puzzled expression crossing his face, then replied, "Are you one of those Ren Faire types? I think you're just pulling my leg."

"Just joking around," Bud replied lamely. "I was hoping you'd found who messed up the rail. But I need to go, nice talking to you, Mister..."

"Rollie O'Reilly. I live up in Helper. I'm an independent rep and work for both D&RGW and Union Pacific, whoever needs me."

"Well, Mister O'Reilly, if you're ever back down this way, look me up and I'll buy you a cup of coffee. My wife owns the Melon Rind Cafe just down the street."

Rollie nodded congenially as Bud headed over to where Howie, looking frustrated, was trying to untangle a long braid of electrical cords. Bud sat down near him.

"Need some help?"

Howie looked up, surprised, then smiled. "Sheriff! Glad you could come! Grab the other end of this and help me out."

As they untangled the cords, Bud asked, "How soon you guys playing, Howie? Do I have time to go home and check on the dogs?"

Howie sounded miffed. "They have us clear at the end of everything, Sheriff. They'll have to wake me up to get started. The event organizer, Susie, said they want us to play last so people will stick around and dance. And they have some other band playing before us. It kind of steals our thunder, if you ask me."

"Well," Bud replied, "Seems to me all the big bands have somebody play before they come on stage. Kind of loosens everyone up for the big performance."

"You think so? The only good thing is it gives us a couple of hours to practice. We haven't got together for weeks, so that will be good."

"Where do you practice, especially if you're already set up here?" Bud asked.

"We just play cold, no electricity, over behind the stage. Maureen hums the piano parts while playing piano on her lap and I play my air guitar."

"And you can hear what you're doing?"

"Not really, but it limbers up the fingers."

"Where's Jimmy?"

"His dad grounded him for staying out all night. They won't be here."

"That's too bad," Bud replied. "Will your friend Cassie Rose make it?"

Like his earlier Viking comment to Rollie, Bud quickly wished he hadn't said anything, but Howie didn't bat an eye.

"Nah, she doesn't like the kind of music we play. But Sheriff, wanna hear the song I wrote for the big occasion?"

Bud again wondered what was going on. Surely Howie would be embarrassed when Bud mentioned Cassie if something was going on.

Bud replied, "I would definitely like to hear it, Howie, especially since I won't be here. That's way too late for me."

Bud hoped Howie would take the news well, especially since he'd promised him he would hang around.

"It's OK, Bud. I'm realizing I was probably being paranoid about all that Viking stuff. Besides, I'm going to stand in the back kind of behind Barry."

Bud laughed as Howie picked up his guitar and started strumming and singing.

> She's something from a dream,
> Even though she's a boy.
> Over one million pounds,
> She for sure ain't no toy.
> And her whistle, it's a beaut,
> You can hear it for miles.
> Everybody stops to listen,
> She brings nothing but smiles.
>
> So, look who's baaaack.
> Spewing cinders on the track.
> Engine 4014,
> Hear the clickity clack.
>
> She's a thing of real beauty,
> A thing so rare.
> Though her steam soaks your clothes,
> She's a breath of fresh air.
> Turns everything black,

But nobody minds,
She's a true work of art,
Truly one of a kind.

So, guess who's baaaack?
Blowing steam from her stack.
It's Engine 4014,
Heed the clickity clack.

Fresh-packed axle bearings,
One-hundred feet long.
A real force of Nature,
Like that old Guthrie song.
Big Steam with a vengeance,
A railfan's joy.
It's OK to stop and stare
At U.P.'s Big Boy.

So, guess who's baaaack?
Diesel engines ain't worth smack.
On her way from Cheyenne,
Love that clickity clack.

Bud clapped, saying, "Howie, that's fantastic! You're going to be a big hit tonight."

Howie looked pleased. "I hope people stick around long enough to hear it."

"It should be the theme song for the event," Bud replied. "You should play it at the opening of the festivities."

"I agree," said a voice behind them. "I couldn't hear it very well, but what I heard was great. Excuse me for eavesdropping."

It was Rollie O'Reilly.

He added, "I'm the U.P. rep here, and I'm going to see if we can open with it. Can you be ready in about an hour?"

Howie grinned, then replied nervously, "I think so. My wife and

Barry can help." He nodded to where Maureen was talking to Barry behind the stage. "We can finish getting set up right away."

Bud grinned. "I may just stick around if it's only going to be an hour. I'm kind of hungry for a funnel cake. I'll help you get set up, then go get us all a snack."

"I'll come back after I talk to Susie," Rollie said. "I can help, too."

Bud grinned. He knew Howie was on his way to fame and fortune, and he probably wouldn't need to raise peanuts to get rich after all.

26

Bud and Howie sat eating funnel cakes, waiting for the event to begin, the stage now set up and ready.

Bud thought back on Howie's song.

"How can it be a Big Boy and yet be a she, Howie?"

"All engines are she's, Bud, like ships. Don't ask me why," Howie replied. "Speaking of ships, have you seen any Vikings around?"

"I saw the wedding couple over by the Loki missiles," Bud answered, referring to the small missiles that stood near the Athena. "They had a bunch of friends with them. Probably the wedding party. Astrid and Arne were holding hands."

"Do you think those are their real names, Bud?"

"Probably not," Bud answered. "They're probably something like Elizabeth and John, popular baby names."

"Did they look like they were in a pillaging mood?"

"Actually, they looked perfectly normal. Just a bunch of young people dressed in shorts and t-shirts and such, though one of them wore a shirt that read, *Gar-Denas Rock*, whatever that means."

Howie asked. "Probably a misspelling of gardener. Was that guy Erik there?"

"No," Bud replied. "I think he was back at the Prickly Pear soaking in baking soda. Sigurd wasn't around, either."

Just then, Susie took to the stage and announced the official start of Big Boy Daze. After telling everyone the train's schedule for the following day and going through a few thank you's to sponsors, especially Union Pacific Railways, she introduced Howie and the Ramblin' Road Rangers, who were now going to play the official Big Boy song. This would be followed by a concert with Hank Williams and Patsy Cline, then Howie and the Ramblin' Road Rangers would finish things out.

Bud figured she'd hired some DJ to play Hank Williams and Patsy Cline records, and he wondered why not just have Howie's band continue playing, since it was live—one would think that would be much better than listening to recordings. He'd heard Wilma Jean say a few things in private about Susie's organizational skills.

The song was a big hit, and the crowd wanted an encore, so Howie and the Ramblin' Road Rangers just continued playing. Bud could see Susie in the back waving at the band, and she looked like she was chafing at the bit, along with some guy next to her, who Bud figured was the DJ.

Howie just ignored her, and the crowd was soon dancing along. Bud thought they sounded pretty good for not having practiced. Rollie the train man was in the front, doing some kind of two-step that reminded Bud of an Irish jig.

Bud now slipped away. His leg was getting more itchy, and he wanted to go home and put some salve on it, as well as see the dogs. He knew Wilma Jean would be at the cafe until late, since Maureen was playing with the band.

He first decided to walk over where he'd seen the Vikings and see if he could find Bjorn's son. He knew time was running out, as the engine would be coming through tomorrow, and after that, everyone would probably leave.

Astrid and Arne sat in the grass, listening to the band, as their friends all danced. Bud wondered if they weren't tired from all the wedding festivities.

Bud soon saw a young guy who he was sure had to be Bjorn's son, as he looked just like him. He was the one wearing the t-shirt with the misspelled words *Gar-Denas Rock*. As the song ended, Bud went over and introduced himself.

"I'm Deputy Bud Shumway, and I'm wondering if I could have a few minutes of your time," he said.

"Sure," the guy shrugged, following Bud to a nearby picnic table. "Did I do something wrong and not realize it, officer?"

Bud laughed. "No, you didn't do anything wrong, not that I'm aware of, anyway. Are you Bjorn Ironside's son, I mean Jim Watson?"

The young man looked away, then answered quietly, "Yes."

"I'm really sorry about what happened. Could I get your name?"

"My real name or my Viking name?"

"Your real name," Bud replied.

"Cory Watson. But I really don't want to have anything to do with my dad. He pretty much abandoned me and my mom."

Bud sighed. "I'm really sorry to bring all this up, but I'm investigating his death."

"It was an accident," Cory said. "That airplane dropped a box that hit him on the head."

"Do you know anyone who saw it happen?"

"Sigurd. He said he did. Erik was with him, too."

"Cory, do you know anything about some kind of dealings between your dad and Erik's grandfather? Could you maybe elaborate what happened?"

"That was a long time ago, before I was even born, and it wasn't my dad, it was my dad's grandfather. It was just like my dad to find something long gone and make a big deal over it. Any kind of drama to distract people from the fact he spent his money on alcohol. My dad decided to be all mad about it, but it was just business."

"What kind of business?"

"It had to do with my great-grandfather suing the Inuit Pie Company, which Erik's grandfather owned. He said they stole his idea for an ice-cream bar. He lost. My dad held a grudge and wouldn't let it go. He said Erik's grandfather stole my family's wealth, but the truth is, we never had any to steal."

"And Sigurd is your uncle?" Bud asked.

"I guess, he's my dad's half-brother. Maybe half-uncle would be more like it."

"Did he and your dad get along?"

"Sometimes. My dad was a real pain, and Sigurd put up with him, but why, I don't know. Sigurd was the only reason my mom and I didn't starve to death."

Bud could tell Cory was getting restless, but he couldn't stop now. He might never have the chance to ask him anything again.

"Did your dad and Sigurd have any kind of business dealings?"

"Not that I know of," Cory replied.

"Would Sigurd have any reason to kill your dad?"

Cory looked shocked. "Kill my dad? Sigurd? No, not at all. He had plenty of reasons, but he's not the type. He was always good to my dad, though he wasn't beneath telling him what he thought of him. Do you have reason to think he did?"

"No," Bud answered quietly. "I'm just covering all the bases. What's Sigurd's real name?"

"Ken Nielson."

"Nielson? That sounds Scandinavian."

"It was his dad's side. My grandma remarried after my grandpa died. He was her second husband. Sigurd is part-Swedish. He's the one who came up with the Ragnarite Society idea and all the Viking stuff. My dad was really into it. It fit my dad's personality—go on the rampage and never apologize. Erik was a Nelson, and Erik and Bjorn spent hours talking about the difference between Nelson and Nielson. Bjorn said Nelson came from the Scandinavian Nielson, but the truth was, Nielson was from the Anglo-Saxon Nelson. Bjorn hated that. Like I said, he'd make a big deal out of nothing."

"Were they related?"

"Not that I know of."

"Did your dad mention anything about messing around with the railroad tracks here?"

Cory looked embarrassed. "He told me he'd done something stupid, but he didn't say exactly what. See, he was totally against Liz and John getting married."

"Elizabeth and John? Astrid and Arne?"

Cory replied, "Yes. My dad said he'd tried to do something to stop the trains from coming through. He knew they were coming on Amtrak."

"He was going to derail their train?" Bud asked.

"No, he knew there would be freight trains coming before them, and one of those would derail and stop everything."

"Interesting. Are you guys going to be around very much longer, Cory?"

Cory sighed, and Bud knew the interview was coming to an end.

"We're leaving in a few days. We want to see Big Boy, then we're going back to California."

Bud stood, holding his hand out and shaking Cory's.

"Cory, you've been very helpful. I really appreciate it. Can I get some kind of contact number in case I need to call you again? Here's my business card—call me anytime if there's anything I can do for you."

Bud handed Cory his card.

"Krider's Melon Farms?" Cory asked. "I thought you were a deputy."

"The farm was my previous job," Bud replied. "Actually, I still work there, but it's ending, though my number will still be the same. The sheriff deputized me for this case. But say, Cory, what do the words on your shirt mean?"

Cory asked, "*Gar-Denas Rock*? It means Vikings Rock! Gar-Dena were the Vikings. It's the first line of *Beowulf.* 'Hwæt! We Gar-Dena in gear-dagum...' It's Old English and means, 'Lo, we the Spear Danes, in days of yore.' The Spear-Danes were the Danish, the Vikings. *Gar* means war in Old English. Like the word *vinegar* means war of the vines, *vine* plus *gar*, because it's so bitter."

"Interesting," Bud replied, feeling as if he'd missed something in his high-school English class.

Bud asked, "But why did Vikings write poetry in Old English? Shouldn't it have been in whatever their language was, something like Old Norse?"

"I think the English maybe translated it from the Old Norse because they liked the poem, seeing how the Vikings were in a lot of hot water with the monster Grendel," Cory answered. "I'm not really into Viking stuff that much. I like science. You guys have some cool rockets there in the park. That's why Sigurd picked Green River. He knew about the Loki missiles here, and he's all into Loki, and he wanted to make a Viking ship so Liz and John could have a Viking wedding, and the Green River was perfect for floating it. We actually had a really good time."

"Are Liz and John into the Viking thing?"

"Not much. They enjoyed the wedding, though. And Sigurd insisted we put my dad's ashes on a little boat someone made out of old boards and float it on down the river, setting it on fire like a Viking funeral."

"You set the boat on fire?" Bud asked, thinking of the smoke he'd seen. He now recalled Howie talking about how Vikings always set boats on fire.

"It was actually pretty cool, except for the fact my dad's ashes were on it."

Bud stood and said goodbye to Cory. As he walked across the park, he could hear Howie and his band playing up a storm.

He got into his FJ and headed for the bungalow, his head spinning. He wondered if Erik's grandfather had indeed stolen the idea for Inuit Pie ice-cream bars and if Krider's farm had been purchased with the proceeds. His thoughts then turned to the missing deed, and to wondering if the Vikings were responsible for the fire down on the Green.

It was all too much, and he looked forward to hanging around with the boys, kicking back and maybe reading for awhile.

Once home, he fed the dogs and slipped into his pajamas, made a cup of peppermint tea, then got comfortable in his big recliner, the dogs nearby, contentedly chewing on their biscuits.

He picked up a newsletter he'd just received from the Museum of the Rockies up in Montana. He'd signed up for their publications when he and Wilma Jean had visited on a trip up there some time ago.

He now read about how museum paleontologist Jack Horner was getting ready to use DNA from a chicken to replicate a real-live dinosaur, since the birds were descendants of the thunder lizards.

Bud shook his head, kind of hoping the experiment wasn't successful. He'd personally found a number of petrified dinosaur tracks out in the desert and knew the beasts weren't something he wanted to have to watch out for when he went out with the dogs. Vikings were bad enough, he mused.

Finally done with the article and glad he didn't live near the museum, Bud turned out the light and dozed off, waiting for Wilma Jean to come home.

27

Bud was back on the farm in the equipment shed, cleaning the place up in preparation for winter, getting the grease off the floors and tidying up the tool boxes.

He'd kind of gotten into the idea of being a deputy for the past few days, but now it was time to do what he was actually being paid to do, manage Krider's farm. Kale was out on a tractor, plowing the fields under, getting them ready for the long cold days ahead.

Bud knew that, like him, Kale looked forward to winter when he could relax, though he also worried about his income when not working. Bud, as manager, had a year-round income, though he figured that would soon be ending.

Howie had called to relay the news that the coroner had finally gotten back to him, and that Bjorn had indeed been killed by something hitting him in the head, but there had been numerous blows.

"If there were multiple blows, Howie," Bud said, "Then Bjorn wasn't killed by just the box, if it even struck him at all. It had to be something else."

"I really examined that box," Howie replied. "And Bud, there wasn't a hint of blood anywhere."

"I'm not surprised, Howie," Bud said. "Since it probably didn't hit Bjorn."

Bud then asked Howie how the rest of the previous night had gone, and Howie replied, "It went fine, Bud, but we finally had to give the stage over to the other guy, you know, the one who was going to do the Hank Williams and Patsy Cline concerts. That was really something, Sheriff. Did you know you can still go on tour after you're dead and make good money?"

"Sounds too easy," Bud replied.

"Well, when Susie announced Hank Williams was coming on stage, nobody believed what they saw—exactly that, Hank Williams coming up onto the stage. He talked to everyone awhile, then started singing *Your Cheatin' Heart*."

"They had an impersonator?" Bud asked.

"No, nobody could do an impersonation like that. It was the real Hank Williams," Howie had replied. "And after he left the stage, same deal with Patsy Cline. Man, she's something else."

"And they weren't impersonators? How did that work?"

"Well, Bud, that fellow we saw in the back with Susie—he's a hologram technician. He puts these concerts together using film footage, doctors them up so they look real, all 3-D and everything, even uses talking and singing from old recordings. It's really cool, but I don't know how my band's going to be able to compete with people like that if they make a comeback."

Bud assured Howie it probably wouldn't be a problem. As they were getting ready to hang up, Howie added, "Say, one other thing the coroner said. He told me that Bjorn's boots were really messed up. It looked like someone had worn them and they didn't fit, way too small. He said they were all bent out of shape and down at the heel."

"Did he save them for us?" Bud asked, knowing Bjorn had been cremated.

"He did. I have them right here," Howie said. "Do you think they might be some kind of evidence?"

Bud thought back to the Wellington boot tracks he'd seen on the cliffs. "They might be, Howie," he replied. "I'll come get them later today. Did he say if he'd found the wedding ring?"

"I almost forgot. He said he'd looked for it in Bjorn's pockets, but couldn't find it. Oh, and he found some kind of old newspaper clipping in his pocket and sent that up, too. But Bud, have you given any more thought to coming back on the force?"

"I'll have to wait and see what's shaking out here, Howie, before I can think about that."

He hung up just in time for Wilma Jean to call and inform him that she and Krider had made a deal on the farm, and it would be theirs that very day. Krider had agreed to do an owner carry.

She'd already sent him a down payment, and his attorney would seal the deal and close on it that afternoon, sending the papers by fax for them to sign and return. The farm would be theirs by late afternoon.

Bud was shocked. He climbed up on the tractor he'd been working on and sat on the seat, absent-mindedly clicking a ballpoint pen from the workbench on and off, over and over. He'd given up on the baton—for something that big, he was sure having trouble keeping track of it. He needed something that fit in his pocket, he mused.

Actually, maybe he needed something stronger than fiddling— maybe a cigarette, even though he'd quit smoking years ago when he'd become a uranium miner. Maybe he should take up chewing Dentine gum again, though he wasn't sure if they even still made it.

Wilma Jean had already signed Kale and Molly on to run the B&B, and she was starting to advertise. They even had people staying there for the next few nights, and Bud guessed they were Big Boy rail-fans. He hoped they wouldn't destroy any walls.

Bud climbed down off the tractor, wandered aimlessly around the shop for a bit, picking up tools and putting them back down, then, giving up on accomplishing anything, took the boys out to the now-dry irrigation ditch.

Sitting under the big cottonwood, he thought of how just a few days ago he'd figured it would be his last time playing stick, and yet it now looked like it might be something they could do clear into old age.

It was a difficult concept for him to grasp, and he knew it would take some time to get used to the fact that he and his wife would soon own the farm, and he could do whatever he wanted here.

Maybe they should donate a few acres for an animal shelter, he thought, since Green River didn't have one, but he wasn't sure how that would work if they didn't yet own it free and clear. He knew Wilma Jean was already planning on building a small airstrip next to one of the fields where she could fly in and out without having to go clear out to the airport.

Bud wondered how they would manage everything, not just time-wise, but financially. He knew Wilma Jean had gone over all the farm's financials with Krider and come up with a payment plan that seemed to work, and since Krider would carry the financing, he knew that if they got into a bind Krider would work with them, unlike a bank.

All in all, it couldn't have been a better deal, Bud mused, and yet he again felt uneasy and almost like running away. He didn't think it was just from any new responsibility, but he wasn't sure. All he knew was that suddenly, instead of feeling excited at co-owning the farm, he almost felt sad, like he was losing his freedom or something.

He now thought back to what the coroner had said about Bjorn's boots and wondered if someone hadn't used them after Bjorn was dead, then put them back on Bjorn's feet. But why?

Bud had come up with a working hypothesis about Bjorn's death, but it was still pretty rough around the edges. Maybe Bjorn had taken the box of Inuit Pies up onto the cliff's edge, then tried to push them off, but had instead gone off with them, losing his balance.

Bud knew that the theory was flawed from the git-go, but he hadn't been able to come up with anything else that worked. Maybe Bjorn was trying to kill Sigurd and make it look like Erik had something to do with it because of the box of Inuit Pies. Or maybe Bjorn had fallen and Erik or Sigurd had hit him, making sure he was dead.

Nothing made sense, and maybe it was time to just give it all up.

Maybe it was an accident like everyone was saying, and Bud should get back to focusing on the farm, now that it would soon be theirs.

He leaned back against the big furrowed trunk of the cottonwood, looking up into the golden leaves, thinking about just wandering around the desert with the boys and his camera, when he heard a distant sound unlike anything he'd ever heard.

For a brief moment he thought of Jack Horner's dinosaurs, then he realized he was hearing the whistle of a steam train far in the distance. It had a sweet melodic sound, and Bud quickly jumped up and headed for the FJ.

Big Boy had finally come to Green River, though a few hours late, and Bud had no intention of missing out on seeing the King of Steam, the mechanical wonder that made grown men weep with joy, even though he hadn't even known it existed until just a few days ago.

"It's alive! Look closely—it breathes, it's self aware. It's beyond a machine, it's a force of Nature!"

Bud didn't know the woman in front of him or where she was from, but he had to agree with her.

Union Pacific Big Boy No. 4014 seemed like a living beast, especially as ethereal steam swirled around the drivers of the giant engine where it stood on a siding at the Green River station, puffing out steam, surrounded by railfans and people who had come hundreds of miles or more to see the huge beast.

Behind the engine sat six passenger cars—vista domes and sleepers—which Bud had heard one could ride from Cheyenne to Ogden for a mere $2,000 apiece. The passengers had gotten off to explore around town or have dinner, as the train would sit there for what was left of the day and all night before heading on up the line in the morning.

Now a small man standing near Bud turned to him and said, "Big Boy doesn't look natural. He wasn't built to pull passenger coaches—he needs a freight train!"

A voice behind him replied, "Right answer. 4014 is made to do the work of several diesels. Some old-timers say they've seen these engines pulling over a mile of freight. Let her do what she was born to do!"

"Long live the king," boomed a voice from the crowd that Bud thought sounded a lot like Billy's, making everyone cheer.

In response, the engineer, who was leaning out the window watching the crowd, blew the whistle several times. Bud was again amazed at how enthralling the sound was.

He now saw Rollie walking along the tracks, wearing a yellow vest with the words, *Union Pacific*, making sure people didn't get too close. When Rollie saw Bud, he waved and came over.

"It's really something, isn't it?" Rollie asked.

Bud agreed as Rollie continued. "The engine weighs 772,250 pounds and the tender is 436,500, and together they outweigh a Boeing 747."

"Why did they need such a big engine?" Bud asked.

"It was built to get freight over the Wasatch Mountains between Green River, Wyoming, and Ogden, Utah. Union Pacific was having to double header and put helper engines on the trains, as the grade was too much. So, in the 1930s, they started working on what would become Big Boy. It was supposed to be called the *Wasatch*, but was called *Big Boy* after someone scrawled the name in chalk on the front of the first one. They built 25 of them between 1941 and 1945, but most are now in the scrap heap of time."

A small group had formed around Bud and Rollie, listening in.

"It's longer than two buses and had to be articulated to make some of the tighter curves. Notice how the exhaust steam from the stack flows over the boiler? That was the reason for U.P. to come up with smoke wings or elephant ears."

Rollie continued talking, getting more and more technical, and as more people gathered around, Bud finally nodded to him and slipped away.

He was glad he'd come down to see the engine, even though he'd had to park a good half-mile away, but the crowds were starting to get to him, and he had other things he needed to do, one being to go to the grocery store.

There was no parking by the Melon Harvest, even though Sherwyn had put up several hand-written signs reading, *Reserved for Our Customers.* Bud would just have to carry his groceries back to the FJ, which was parked clear over by the Chow Down.

"Morning, Sherwyn," he said, greeting the owner as he went in. The store was empty, in spite of the full parking lot. "Looks like the railfans have taken over the whole town."

Sherwyn shook his head. "I'm just trying to stay positive, Bud, hoping they'll all come buy groceries when the train leaves."

Bud got a cart and began making the rounds, being sure to pick up several boxes of Barkie Biscuits. He then headed for the ice-cream isle, wanting to get some vanilla-bean for his coffee, but then decided it would melt by the time he got it home, since he'd have to walk so far.

He went back to the front and asked, "Say, Sherwyn, do you have any dry ice if I should get some ice cream? I'm parked about a quarter-mile away and it's going to melt."

"I do," Sherwyn replied, "Though your wife about wiped me out the other day."

"Wilma Jean?"

"Yeah, she got a big bunch to pack around the box of Inuit Pies she bought. Wiped me out of those, too," Sherwyn replied. "I usually don't sell them by the carton, but she said she was supplying some wedding party or something. I was thinking that was pretty cheap, most people have nice cakes, but who am I to question it? Was it a friend of hers or something?"

"No, it was an air drop out by the river."

"Oh, now that makes sense. A cake would fall flatter than a pancake if you dropped it from a plane. Speaking of river, have you heard about the fire? It's totally out of control. The BLM has called for help and some regional fire crews are coming in. It's coming upriver with all that dry vegetation on the river bottoms, but it's trying to jump out of the canyon."

Bud sighed. "I wouldn't think there would be that much to burn, but it's fall and everything's drying up. I hope they get it under control."

"A hotshot crew came in here this morning for supplies and said there's fear it's going to hit town, come on up to some of the farms and hit the state park and golf course. That's green enough it probably wouldn't burn, but those houses along there might, one of them being Sheriff McPherson's."

"Would your house be in danger?" Bud asked, knowing Sherwyn lived just around the corner from Howie.

"It might, but only if it was so out of control that town caught fire. There's a good block of houses between me and him."

"We need to stay informed," Bud replied. "Since I'm no longer on the force, it's hard for me to keep track of what's going on."

"I have my scanner," Sherwyn replied. "Actually, Bud, you know a lot of people here bought scanners after you quit. Sheriff McPherson's doing a good job, better than a lot of people initially thought he would, but we miss you more than you'll ever know."

"Thanks, Sherwyn, I appreciate that," Bud replied, his cart now full, including two gallons of vanilla-bean ice cream. He'd thrown a couple of heads of lettuce in to help balance it out.

As Sherwyn checked him out, Bud asked, "Do you mind if I take this cart off the premises? I kind of got carried away, and there's no way I can carry all this. I can put it in my FJ and bring it back later."

"Not a problem," Sherwyn replied. "I'll wrap that ice cream in dry ice. But you know, I've been thinking, Krider's Farm is right in the path of that fire if it keeps coming north. You might want to batten down the hatches."

"Good idea," Bud replied. "I never figured it would get that far, but who knows? Thanks for the reminder."

With that, Bud headed out the door, pushing the cart full of groceries along the streets of Green River Town, nodding at friends and neighbors as they drove by, wondering if living out of a grocery cart might be his future if they couldn't make things work out on the farm.

29

Bud sat at Howie's desk, thinking back when he was sheriff and spent a lot of time in this exact same place and position. He noticed the desk was piled with old *Lost Treasure* magazines and wondered if any of his old photography magazines were still around.

He thought for a moment about what it would be like to be sheriff again, then sighed, as it didn't seem very likely, now that he and Wilma Jean had signed the contract on the Krider farm. He guessed the townspeople would start calling it the Shumway farm from now on, unless Erik found that deed.

Bud wondered where Howie was, though he knew he was busy with all the railfans in town. Instead of entertaining them, he was probably now detaining them, Bud smiled.

Howie had told Bud where to find Bjorn's boots and the newspaper article from Bjorn's pocket, then said he'd be there just as soon as he finished lecturing some kids about getting into one of Big Boy's passenger cars and trying to hide so they could ride the train. The kids had apparently been hiding for hours when they realized the train wasn't going anywhere and had been spotted by the conductor.

Bud now carefully read the article from Bjorn's pocket as he waited for Howie. It was from the *San Francisco Tribune* and dated several months earlier.

Invaluable Viking Ring Stolen from Museum

One of the most unique rings in history, dated from about 900 A.D., has been stolen from a traveling display of the National Museum of Denmark. The ring was securely housed in the San Diego Museum of Man, along with the complete Viking Hoard from Terslev in Zealand.

The hoard also contained numerous silver coins, the latest from the year 944, as well as silver neck and arm rings, a silver drinking service with four Nordic cups, and a large embossed silver bowl. None of these were touched by the thief, who took only the ring, which was said to be the most valuable item in the hoard.

Silver was the most important precious metal of the Viking Age and came to Scandinavia by various routes controlled by Swedish Vikings. These Viking hoards, of which there were many, provide evidence of the Vikings' activities abroad, as many of the hoards contain objects that came from faraway places.

The stolen ring is called "Hrothgar's Secret," and is said to exhibit the finest craftsmanship ever seen in a Viking piece. The ring is decorated with runes, but no one's ever been able to decipher their meaning. Some experts feel that this is because the runes were simply used to disguise the ring's deeper display and actually have no meaning.

The runes were incised into the silver ring using a technology never seen before or after, using a fine-tipped tool to make points of varying depth. When viewed in normal light, one sees the runes, but supposedly when viewed in muted sunlight at the perfect angle, something different appears. Since no one has seen the ring in its perfect lighting, it's uncertain what actually appears, thus the name, Hrothgar's Secret, after the Viking leader who supposedly had the ring made, though some question his existence. Viking mythology indicates that the ring contained the secret to happiness. A number of light technicians have tried to reveal the ring's secret, but none have succeeded.

Police have fingerprints, but so far, there are no suspects and no arrest has been made.

Bud whistled. Was this the ring that Wilma Jean had in the box on her plane? It sure sounded like it. And so much for it being in the family for 1,000 years—it sounded to Bud like it had become part of the family much more recently.

He wondered what had happened to it and found it odd that no one seemed very concerned when it was stolen from the plane. Maybe they were regretting taking it from the museum and were worried they'd get caught.

And he wondered how one could possibly carve the secret to happiness in the diameter of a small ring.

Just then, Howie came in, and Bud showed him the article.

"Whooee, Sheriff," Howie said. "Do you think that's the same ring that they were going to use for the wedding?"

"I'm pretty sure it is, Howie," Bud replied. "For Bjorn to be carrying a newspaper article about it in his pocket, well, that indicates to me a connection."

"Makes sense," Howie said. "But hey, Bud, I need to clean out all these magazines. Any idea who might want them?"

Bud was surprised. "Maybe the library, but why get rid of them?" Bud knew Howie enjoyed reading them when things got slow.

"The mayor came by and said they didn't reflect well on my duties," Howie replied. "Apparently people come in and think all I do is sit around reading them."

Howie picked one up and thumbed through it, looking upset, then said, "They give people something to do when they come in and I'm busy and can't get to them right away. I mean, just the other day, Junkyard Goldie came in to complain about something or other and I was on the phone trying to calm Mrs. Jensen down, as another kid had ridden his dirt bike across her lawn, and by the time I got off the phone, Goldie was so busy reading about some place where Butch Cassidy had supposedly buried some gold coins that he forgot what he'd come in to complain about. We had a nice visit and Goldie went on over to the library to see if he could do some research on it. So, they actually do serve a purpose, Sheriff."

Bud replied, "Oh, I know, Howie. Besides, no point in just staring at the wall when nothing's going on."

Howie replied, "I found a couple of *Outdoor Photographer* magazines under your desk after you left. I kept forgetting to get them back to you, and now I can't remember what I did with them. One was about taking photos of stars and the Milky Way and it kind of got me started in getting a good camera and doing deep-sky photography."

"Photography magazines under my desk?" Bud snorted. "Probably the cleaning lady's."

"Nope, not the cleaning lady's," Howie said. "Since that would be me. But Bud, have you heard about this fire coming up the river? I've been monitoring it on the radio, and it's starting to sound serious."

"It is," Bud agreed. "But there's not much you and I can do, except be ready to evacuate. Do you have a plan for getting everything you need and the cats out if it gets too close? You can always come out to our place."

"I've already packed up my guitar equipment and taken it to the drive-in," Howie replied. "And Maureen's got her stuff ready. We have cat carriers and keep the cats inside so we can find them if we need to leave. There's a little white bunny that's been hanging around, and it's getting to where it will let me catch it, so I would hope to take it, too. I think it's someone's lost pet. And thanks, Bud, I appreciate the offer. I hope we don't have to take you up on it."

Howie sighed, then added, "I'll sure be glad when this train's gone. I mean, it's totally something else, but there's too many people in town, Bud. And I need to finish up this thing I'm..." Howie stopped.

"Thing? What kind of thing?"

Howie seemed suddenly reticent, but said, "I've been going out to Cassie Rose's house a lot, but I'm pretty much done. It'll be nice to have my evenings back."

Bud sat quietly, not sure what to say, but just then Howie's phone rang and he had to go out on another call, leaving Bud feeling desultory again, wondering what his good buddy was up to.

It was then that he noticed the camp chair, still in the corner where he'd left it. He again tried to open it up, but this time he succeeded, though he kind of wished he hadn't, for the canvas fabric was covered in dried blood.

Bud now felt a mixture of elation and disgust, for he knew he'd found what had really killed Bjorn. Someone had used the folded-up camp chair as a weapon, and he now knew for certain that the box of Inuit Pies hadn't fallen on Bjorn at all, but the chair had been used to hit Bjorn on the head.

It was an unhappy discovery, yet Bud knew that it was possible that the chair had fingerprints that could implicate the murderer. He would ship it off to the lab in the morning.

Bud finally got up and left, locking the door behind him, Bjorn's boots in an evidence bag under his arm.

30

Bud was putting the groceries away, glad that Sherwyn had wrapped the ice cream in dry ice since it had taken him longer to get home than he'd anticipated.

He stuck the two gallons into the freezer, noticing that Wilma Jean had left him a note on the counter.

Bud, Krider's wife found dead. Call me. XXOO WJ

Bud was stunned. Krider's wife found dead? What had happened? Was it from natural causes, or had something bad happened? And just when she'd gone back home to be with her elderly parents. Bud quickly dialed his wife's number.

"Hi, hon," she answered, sounding her normal cheerful self.

"I got your note," Bud replied. "I'm sorry to hear it."

"What? Why?" Wilma Jean asked, perplexed.

"Do you know what happened? Will Krider be OK? Do you think he might want to return out here? Would he want the farm back, you think?"

"Bud Shumway, whatever are you talking about?"

"Your note said, and I quote, 'Krider's wife found dead.' I don't know what to say. Should I call him?"

Wilma Jean broke out laughing, and Bud thought it must be a reaction from the stress.

"You okay?" He asked.

"Bud, Bud, Bud," she replied. "Sometimes I don't know whether to laugh or to cry. I wish you could see me shaking my head. What a difference one letter makes. Substitute an *e* for the *a* in the last word, and see what you get."

Bud studied the note again. Finally, he said quietly, "Deed. Krider's wife found deed."

"Correct," she replied, her tone reminding Bud of one of his grade-school teachers.

"Well, what now?" He asked. "Was the farm legally Krider's to sell?" Bud was kind of half-hoping it wasn't.

"She found it quite some time ago, while renovating the house. I mean, this was a long time ago, hon, when they first bought it. She took it to a real-estate attorney in Price, and he went to the title company over in Castle Dale, and it was deemed invalid. When Mr. Nelson signed the farm over to the Thaynes, who the Kriders later bought it from, the deed was made invalid by the bill of sale and a new deed was issued. These things happen more than you'd think, where a legal document doesn't get turned in or processed properly and people try to claim the property, at least that's what the attorney said. It's all legal and square, Bud. No worries."

Bud sighed. "And Mrs. Krider's OK?"

"As far as I know," she laughed again.

"Good. Good. Are you coming home soon?" Bud looked at the dog clock on the wall. It read 5:30, the dog's tail clicking back and forth.

"I have an air drop as soon as I can get out of here. The BLM wants me to drop stuff to the firefighters down on the river. The only access is by jetboat, and the fire's making that too dangerous."

"What are you dropping them?"

"A big tub of barbecued beef, buns, and some cold drinks. Oh, and some firefighting equipment."

Bud thought a barbecued beef sandwich sounded really good.

Howie's Drive-In used to have great BBQ sandwiches, and Bud wondered if Howie really would open it again soon.

"Is there any extra?" He asked.

"I'll bring you some when I get back," she replied.

Bud advised, "Be careful. The setting sun might be in your eyes, and going down into the river canyon might be a bit sketchy."

"Don't worry, hon. Vern's going with me."

Bud was glad to hear it, as Vern would make sure everything was fine. His wife still didn't have a lot of flying experience, and Bud knew canyon flying could be tricky because of the air currents, especially around fires. But Vern had done it all and then over again.

"It would be nice to get a report on where the fire is, if you can," Bud said.

"Will do, hon. Gotta run."

Bud finished unloading the groceries, fed the dogs, then turned on a couple of lights, grabbed his keys, and stepped out the door. He wanted to go back out to the site where Bjorn had died, for he felt like he hadn't had the chance to really carefully examine everything. If he hurried, he had just enough time to get there, look around, and at least get back on the road before dark.

Hesitating, he went back inside and grabbed his Ruger and shoulder harness, putting it on.

While putting the groceries away, something had just occurred to Bud, and it made him wonder if he wasn't losing his touch as a detective, though it was maybe something anyone could overlook.

Thinking back to whoever had broken into Wilma Jean's plane—hadn't they strewn camping gear all over the place? He and Howie and Sammy had picked it all up, but it was obviously thrown from the plane in an attempt to find something, and that something had to be the Viking ring.

So why had they all three, himself included, assumed the thief had known where the ring was—simply because he'd managed to find it under the pilot's seat? Any good thief would think to look in such out of the way places, especially since it was such a small item and would fit about anywhere.

This meant that Bjorn could easily have been the thief. Sigurd had given Wilma Jean the ring to be delivered in the air drop with the other stuff, but Bjorn had broken in later, rightly suspecting the ring to be there. And if Bjorn had been the one who'd stolen the ring, he must have felt it was rightfully his.

Bud suspected that the fact that Bjorn was now dead had something to do with the ring, and he had a hunch he might find more if he could just get back out to the site of the air drop before it got dark.

Turning onto Long Street, he felt beneath his seat, pulling out the powerful flashlight he kept there, setting it on the passenger seat.

It would serve to light the way if he took longer than anticipated, Bud thought, and it would also serve as a good weapon, although Bud suspected it wouldn't do much good if he met a heathen Berserker.

31

Bud pulled up near the place where they'd found Bjorn, sat in his FJ for a few minutes, then backed up and parked it behind a rock outcropping where it would be hidden from anyone on the road.

For some reason, his intuition was telling him to be extra cautious, that matters here weren't necessarily over. He got out and walked to the area where Wilma Jean had dropped the camping supplies and began looking around.

The smell of smoke was almost overpowering, and Bud could see where a good portion of the vegetation down along the river had burned, some of it still smoldering. He knew the fire was now burning upriver, and he'd noticed on his way there that the plume of smoke seemed to be very close to town. Hopefully, Wilma Jean would bring back a report.

Bud had no idea what he was looking for, and it was very possible there was nothing to find anyway, especially since it had been a few days and any tracks could easily have blown away. He grimaced—he really should've come back out sooner, but as they say, life got in the way.

The drop area was near a wide beach on the river where the

Viking party had camped, but Bud knew there was no reason to go down there, as anything and everything had been obliterated by the fire.

He walked over to where Erik and Sigurd had parked the blue car and looked around there some, studying the various footprints back and forth to the nearby drop site.

So far, all he could see was a mishmash of tracks and gouges in the dirt where they'd dragged camping gear down to the beach.

He next walked over to the small stand of poison oak. He thought of Erik, wondering if he'd recovered. Could this be the stand responsible for Erik's misery? Erik had said he'd gotten into poison oak along the golf course, but Bud didn't know of any poison oak there. Come to think of it, hadn't Erik said he wasn't sure where he got into it? Bud now thought back to his own itchy leg, glad that was over.

Now pulling one of Bjorn's boots from the small pack he was carrying, he studied the boot marks coming out of the bushes. Comparing them to the boots, he was almost certain they were the same. And though it was subtle, he could see where the edges of the boots had pushed into the ground just a little, as if the boots were splayed over by someone whose feet were too big for them. Had someone put Bjorn's boots on?

He could now see something out of place over by a nearby juniper tree, something an off-white, so he walked over to take a look. To his surprise, he found a stick that looked identical to those found in ice-cream bars.

Bud stuck the stick in his pocket, wondering if someone hadn't taken a break for an Inuit Bar before proceeding, as it was something he himself would do. As he paused, looking up to watch a raven, he noticed a branch of the nearby juniper had been torn off. The wood still looked fresh, as if it had happened recently, and he suspected this was the source of the broom someone had used to try to erase their tracks.

He then decided to climb the cliff one last time and see if he'd missed anything, so he walked over to the base of the hill. Checking back to see if he could see his FJ, he was relieved to see it was still hidden, even from this angle.

The tracks were still there, though less obvious, and Bud again took out one of Bjorn's boots to see if they matched, which they did. The edges of the boots were splayed over, just like the tracks coming from the bushes.

Could someone have killed Bjorn and dragged his body over into the poison oak to hide it, then taken off his boots and crammed them onto their own feet, making it look like Bjorn's tracks? They'd then taken the box of Inuit Pies Wilma Jean had dropped for the wedding party and climbed the hill, carrying it. Once on top, they'd dropped the box off the cliff. They could then have dragged the body over by the box and claimed he'd been hit.

Bud shook his head. Like his previous theory, it made no sense. The only reason someone would wear Bjorn's boots was to make it look like he'd been the one to drop the box, yet he was the one who'd been killed.

Bud now sat on a large rock, watching the sun begin its descent into other worlds, bringing dawn and a new day to far-away people who Bud would never know existed. There was enough smoke in the air that he knew it was going to be a spectacular sunset, and he wished he'd brought his camera.

Watching for rattlers, he walked over to the far side of the hill to better think while watching the setting sun. He saw something shining in the dirt, and thought of ravens and how they were attracted to shiny things and had probably brought something up there, for he knew no one would ever have a reason to come up this remote hill in the middle of nowhere.

Reaching down to pick it up, he was stunned to see it was the Viking ring, *Hrothgar's Secret*. It must've fallen from Bjorn's pocket, a raven retrieving it and dropping it here. The odds were astronomical that Bud would find the ring, and yet there it was, the silver gleaming in the sunlight.

As he held the ring up to the light, he wondered if it really held the secret to happiness, and if so, if it would deign to reveal the secret to him, a non-Viking, a lowly farmer who had no idea how he'd come to be on a remote cliff in eastern Utah, holding a thousand-year-old ring from a Viking hoard in Scandinavia.

32

The sun blazed for a moment, then slipped behind a long black haze of smoke on the horizon, turning everything a blood red.

Bud held the ring up, noting the many fine incisions the master craftsman had used to create the runes, hundreds of points for each letter. It must've taken many hours to make each rune, Bud surmised, a true masterpiece.

But as Bud stood on the cliff, the sun slowly setting, he noticed the runes began to slowly disappear, and in their place, something much deeper appeared with a darker hue. As he watched in amazement, the ring began to display something he couldn't quite make out, though it looked like several silver points in a black background.

Bud was disappointed. How could this be the secret to happiness? There was no answer here, just a few points that were maybe supposed to be stars, but with no discernible meaning.

But as he continued to watch, the ring continued to change, until it became obvious that what he was seeing was indeed some kind of scene, though of what he still wasn't sure. He did know he probably had very little time to figure it out, as the ring was already starting to show the faint outlines of the runes as the sun set.

Looking closely, it suddenly dawned on Bud that he was looking at a beautifully done three-dimensional rendering of Polaris, with the Big Dipper pointing to it, as well as several other nearby stars. He thought of Howie and how patiently he'd taught Bud the different constellations.

The ring soon faded back to runes, and Bud stood in wonder, thinking of the Viking that had created it and how difficult it must have been to make the amazing 3D image he'd just seen.

Polaris—the North Star. The Vikings had been the masters of the seas, and they surely knew the night sky like the back of their hands, for astronomical bearings would be the backbone of their wanderings and for successfully reaching their destinations. They'd travelled everywhere, and the North Star was that critical link to the many oceanic paths they followed.

The ring must be a fallback for when one forgot how to find Polaris, though Bud couldn't imagine anyone not knowing how, especially a seafarer.

But then he thought back to the article he'd read about the ring. They'd called it *Hrothgar's Secret*, the secret to happiness.

How could a rendition of a small section of the night sky be the secret to happiness? Bud wasn't sure, but he knew it must have to do with a deep need to wander, to travel, to see the world. Maybe to a Viking, happiness was following the North Star.

It was almost dark, the horizon now a deep smoky purple, and Bud thought back to another wanderer he knew, one just as dedicated to seeing new worlds as any Viking could have been—his uncle over in Colorado's Paradox Valley, who had once been a hobo.

Like his uncle, Bud had always wanted to be free, to wander around and explore the desert, learning the names of all the plants and flowers and animals, as well as the rocks and geologic layers, understanding how the landscape was formed and came to be. It was a freedom that challenged his curiosity as well as his longing to see different places and how others lived, whether they be animal or human.

At one time he'd wished he'd been a train engineer, but he eventually realized he'd be traveling the same lines over and over, a movement that made you think you were advancing when you actually weren't. He knew the feeling must run in the family, as his Uncle Junior had once ridden the rails.

Bud now thought back to something Junior had told him when he was young. Bud had been helping his grandfather on the Preston Nutter Ranch near Price when the two Musser brothers, Jack and Tom, had come over to buy some bulls.

After getting to know them a little, he hitched a ride with them and the bulls back over to their ranch near Delta, Colorado in Escalante Canyon, not to be confused with the one in Utah, even though it had similar redrock formations.

Once there, Bud had worked for them for a week or so until his mom had demanded he come home. Junior had just happened to be in the neighborhood, on his way back from Grand Junction to his general store in Paradox, and Bud's mom had asked him to pick Bud up.

Bud had been all of about 14 years old, though everyone said he was mature for his age, so he'd told the Mussers he was 16.

As they rode back to Utah in Junior's old pickup, Junior had told him, "Buddy boy, I know exactly what you're feeling, as I was the same way at your age, and in fact, I still am. You get the wandering urge and it won't leave you be, it follows you around day and night. I personally have dirt from over 40 states on me, and the only ones missing are the ones with very little dirt 'cause they're all paved over."

Bud had listened well, probably because there was nothing else to do, as the old truck didn't even have a radio. His uncle had a captive audience and knew it.

"Buddy, listen up here. In order to be truly free, you have to give up everything you own. All those hobos out there, those bums, their stories all start the same—leaving home—but none of those stories ever end at home. And that's all they have, is their stories. A lot of them would like to be on their way home, but they ain't got one. They chase around and get chased around in turn, sometimes by the law, but more often by their memories."

Junior looked at Bud, making sure he was listening.

Bud nodded his head, and Junior continued.

"Look out there at that big horizon. It may look real enticing, but it just never ends. You think you finally got somewhere, and there it is, calling you on. And don't forget, the ultimate price for your freedom ain't not having a home, not having anything at all, but instead it's the two things you *do* have—a big hole in your pocket and an unimaginable loneliness."

Bud had studied the dark clouds on the horizon as Junior talked, and for some reason, from then on out, dark clouds like that always made him feel lonely.

Junior had taken Bud home, hung out there for a few days visiting with family, then gone on back to Colorado.

Bud wondered what Junior was doing now. He was probably sitting in front of his old general store in Paradox, eating Inuit Pies, though they'd been called Eskimo Pies back then. He wondered why they'd changed the name and suspected it had something to do with being politically correct.

The sun had now set and darkness began pushing the fading clouds from the sky. Bud stood, turned on his flashlight and slowly walked back down the hill.

It was time to go home, and he felt lucky to have not just one, but two places he could now go to—the bungalow and the farm. Both felt like home, and he was glad for it.

33

As he reached the bottom of the hill, Bud knew his prospects for going home had diminished greatly, for he heard a voice say, "Hold it right there, Bud. Drop the light and put your hands up. You're looking into the muzzle of a gun, even if you can't see it."

Bud could now see two shadows standing nearby. He thought for a second of going for his Ruger, but instead dropped the light and put his hands up, wondering who would know him well enough to call him by name and yet want him incapacitated.

Now the voice said, "This is the guy Erik said wasn't even fazed by a rattlesnake bite."

Bud now recognized the voice. It was Sigurd, and he wasn't alone, unless he was used to talking to himself.

"Maybe he has an immunity to them," the other shadow said, and even though the voice was familiar, Bud wasn't sure who it was.

"How'd you get out here?" Sigurd demanded.

"I came down the river," Bud replied. It was technically true, as the River Road pretty much followed the river, though maybe over a ways. He was glad now he'd hidden the FJ, as it might be his only escape.

"I'm really not into this, Uncle Sigurd. I didn't know you were going to do this."

Bud now recognized the voice as Cory's.

Cory picked up Bud's flashlight and shone it on Sigurd.

Sigurd replied, "You knew we were coming out here for the ring. This guy's been out here snooping around several times. He's a detective and has to have found it."

Bud wondered how Sigurd knew all this, then figured he'd talked to Erik.

"I'm sorry, Mr. Shumway," Cory continued. "If you have the ring, it would be best to give it to Sigurd. He'd leave you be then, right, Sigurd?" Cory pleaded.

"I don't know, it depends on if he cooperates or not. Give Cory the ring, and no funny biz. Keep one hand up, take the ring from your pocket, hand it to Cory, then put it back up."

Cory now shone the light on Bud.

Bud wondered what Sigurd would do if he said he didn't have the ring. He wasn't in the mood to be searched, so he carefully took the ring from his shirt pocket and handed it to Cory, then put his hand back up. He wasn't sure how long he could keep his hands up, because he now had an almost uncontrollable urge to fiddle with something.

Cory handed Sigurd the ring, who tried to examine it in the flashlight's beam.

"Where'd you get this?" He asked.

"It was up on the backside of the hill. I think a raven dropped it there."

Sigurd looked doubtful, then asked, "Ravens do stuff like that?"

Bud replied, "Oh, sure, and even worse. Sometimes they'll drop things on your head. Golf balls, rocks, twigs. But can I put my hands down now? I'm getting tired."

Sigurd, who'd been looking up at the sky in disbelief while trying to watch Bud at the same time, now said, "No. Keep them up. Cory, go get the car and bring it over here."

"I don't have the keys," Cory replied.

Sigurd now put his hand in his pants pocket, trying to get the keys, which seemed stuck. Bud knew he could have pulled his Ruger several times over while Sigurd fumbled around, but he wasn't into gunplay, as he knew someone would get hurt, and it might be him.

Sigurd finally retrieved the keys, and Cory went to get the car.

"Are you a deputy sheriff?" Sigurd now asked Bud.

"I'm a farmer," Bud dodged, not sure how far he should take Howie's deputization. He knew it would probably be for the best to not be involved with law and order right now, considering the unlawful disorder he was dealing with.

"I didn't mean to kill Bjorn," Sigurd now bleated out, sounding like a ten-year-old who'd been caught stealing apples. "He tried to kill me first. He'd stolen the ring, and I was trying to talk him into giving it back for the wedding. He just went berserk and came after me. I whacked him over the head with a camp chair, then when he went down, I just panicked and hit him over and over. I knew if he woke up he would kill me. Bjorn was incredibly strong, that's why we called him Bjorn Ironsides. The original Bjorn Ironsides, back in Viking times, was said to be able to turn a battle singlehandedly."

Bud was shocked. He'd never had anyone confess to a crime while holding *him* at gunpoint. It wasn't in the books, and he wasn't sure what to say.

Finally, he asked, "Did Bjorn steal the ring from the museum?"

"No," Sigurd replied, the gun now sagging—he was obviously getting tired of holding it up. "He bought it from a pawn shop. I think it was fenced—I'm sure it was fenced. He found out later where it was stolen from. He should have returned it, but he was besotted by its Vikingness and the myth that it held the secret to happiness."

Bud could now hear Cory starting the car, and he knew his time with Sigurd was coming to an end. He tried to think of any questions he could ask while Sigurd was being so forthcoming.

Sigurd continued. "He spent hours trying to decipher the runes, to no avail. He got more and more obsessed with the Viking stuff. He would even make up stuff in his mind, like Liz being of royal blood. He finally slipped away and lost all connection with reality."

Sigurd had now forgotten all about the gun, letting it drift down-wards toward Bud's feet.

"When he found out Liz and John were getting married, he offered them the ring. Liz loved it, so we agreed to use it, though she had no idea it was stolen. Then Bjorn decided he wanted it back and stole it from the plane, which was really dumb, because it was his in the first place, as far as I was concerned. I didn't want anything to do with it other than for the wedding. But I didn't worry about it, as I knew he had it. Actually, John, my son, had already bought a beautiful ring for Liz, and they used that for the wedding ceremony."

Bud knew he might be pushing his luck, but he had to ask, "Why do you want the ring now, if you don't want anything to do with it?"

Sigurd sighed. "I found out there's a big reward for it. Since Bjorn isn't around, I figured I could give the money to Cory and his mom. They could sure use it."

Bud had one more question, for he knew his time was almost up.

"Was Erik involved in Bjorn's death? Did he drag him into the poison oak?"

Sigurd replied flatly, "No, I did. I got drunk after the wedding and almost fell into the river, and Erik got the poison oak from catching me, sort of a contact exposure. I did have one night of itching, but I was too drunk to really care. Erik really suffered until he went to the doctor."

Cory now pulled up next to Sigurd and said, "We should give him a ride back, Uncle Sigurd. He gave us the ring, and it's an awfully long walk. I'm going to drive, since you've been drinking."

Sigurd, now holding the gun back up, said to Bud, "Keep your hands up for five minutes after we're gone or I'll shoot."

Bud waited as they drove off, then put his hands down. He wasn't too worried about Sigurd shooting, as they were long gone, their tail-lights fading into the darkness.

He ran to the rocks where the FJ was hidden and was soon following them, all the while fiddling with a small stick from his pocket that bore the words, *Inuit Pie.*

34

Bud had tried to call Howie several times, but with no luck. He was hot on the tail of Sigurd and Cory, but he knew they would beat him back to town, and he wanted backup before things got rough.

He wasn't sure if Sigurd would actually shoot, but he was beginning to consider the Ragnarites to be a pretty crazy bunch. He had no intentions of trying to stop them on his own.

He rounded the corner near the airport road turnoff, and it was then that he saw a plane about to come in for a landing. Considering the lack of air traffic around Green River, he knew it had to be Wilma Jean and Vern.

Pulling his phone from his pocket, he dialed his wife. Sometimes it was hard to make a connection when she was in the air, but he knew the cell service was good near the airport.

"Hello, hon," she answered. "I'll be home soon."

"Can you see me? I'm the second car below you," Bud asked.

"I can," she replied. "What are you doing out here?"

The FJ careened a little as Bud took a curve with one hand. "I'm following that car in front of me. I need to arrest them, but they're armed, and I can't get ahold of Howie."

"Arrest them? For what?"

"Murder."

The phone went silent for awhile, then Bud heard Vern's voice.

"You say they're armed? Pistol or long gun?" He asked.

"Pistol. I couldn't see exactly what kind in the dark. But I gotta go, I'm driving way too fast to be on the phone."

"We'll see what we can do, Bud," Vern said, hanging up.

Bud could now see the plane turn and head back his way, following the road and eventually getting ahead of both him and the car.

Bud was surprised and wondered where they were going. He'd figured they would go ahead and land and then try to find Howie.

The plane was some distance from them when it began to swing back around and start straight toward them. He couldn't believe it! It looked like they were going to land on the road and try to block the car.

Since it was fairly dark, he hoped Vern was at the controls, as he didn't think Wilma Jean had the experience to make such a landing. He knew it would probably be a piece of cake for Vern, who was a grandson of Gas Wells of early canyon aviation fame.

Bud had heard many stories about Gas, short for Gaston, who would land his plane in the field near the little Hanksville grocery store near where they lived, go in and get groceries, then enjoy a cigar in front of the nearby gas station, telling stories about his flying escapades, drumming up business from whoever might want to see the backcountry from the air. His wife Gladys, Vern's grandmother, always said that Gas's name fit him because he was full of hot air.

Most of Gas's wild adventures had actually happened, and though Gas had never wrecked a plane or lost a passenger, many were afraid to fly with him, especially after he'd once landed in Muddy Creek where it exited the San Rafael Reef. Since his engine had died, it was land there or crash. Defying predictions of an early demise, Gas had instead died at the ripe old age of 103 at the Beehive House over in Loa.

If anyone could land that plane on the road in the dark, it was Gas's grandson, Vern, Bud thought. Vern had been one of the few reasons Bud hadn't complained too much when Wilma Jean had said she wanted to take up flying, for with Vern as her instructor, Bud knew she'd be in good hands.

Now the plane was losing altitude, and Bud could see it was on the right trajectory to land on the road. He just hoped Vern didn't overshoot his calculations and actually have a head-on collision with Sigurd and Cory. He decided to pull back a little just in case.

Bud could now see Vern set the plane down onto the road, smooth as could be, a perfect distance for Cory to stop without hitting him. The plane's wings covered both lanes, so there was no chance of going around.

Bud figured Vern and Wilma Jean would stay in the plane, seeing how they knew Sigurd was armed. He wasn't real sure how he was going to make the arrest, but he knew they wouldn't expect him to be in the vehicle behind them, seeing how they'd left him to walk back. He hoped he could use the element of surprise.

Bud quickly pulled up behind them, jumped out, and held his Ruger up to the passenger's open window, saying, "Hands up!"

Vern was quickly out of the plane and at the driver's side, and Bud could see he was armed.

But instead of putting his hands up, Sigurd went for his gun.

Bud quickly pointed the barrel of the Ruger straight at Sigurd, saying, "You might want to toss that on the ground. The nearest hospital's an hour away."

Now Cory grabbed the gun and threw it out the driver's window, and as Vern picked it up, Bud told Sigurd and Cory both to get out.

As they stood there, hands up, leaning against the car, Bud searched them as Vern held them at gunpoint. Bud wasn't sure what to do next, as he didn't have any handcuffs, nor a vehicle with a barrier to take them into town.

"Now what?" Vern asked, fully aware of the problem.

"Maybe I should let them walk back to town," Bud said, eyeing Sigurd.

"We need to take off before it's totally pitch black," Vern said. "We still need to land at the airport, and there're no lights there."

Vern now went over to the plane to talk to Wilma Jean, and he soon returned, saying, "Your wife's going to take the plane back while I stay here with you. Then she'll go find Howie and come back."

"I tried to call him several times," Bud said, wondering if Howie was out at the Rose Ranch. "It's unlike him to not answer."

"We saw him down by the golf course with his lights flashing," Vern replied. "I think he's evacuating that part of town. The fire's totally out of control."

Bud was shocked. Evacuating? He thought of how Sherwyn had reminded him that Krider's farm was in the path of the fire. He needed to get over there and help out. He again eyed Sigurd, who refused to look at him.

"I have to admit I'm worried about my wife flying that plane in the dark," Bud told Vern.

"She'll be OK," Vern replied. "She didn't have any trouble making those canyon air drops, and she landed it here with no trouble, so I think she'll be fine. She's been working on her instrument rating."

Bud hoped that Sammy had turned on the airport lights, such as they were, feeling a mixture of concern and pride as he watched Wilma Jean expertly turn the Cessna around and take off into the wild black yonder, heading for the Green River Airport.

35

Bud sat with his feet up on Howie's desk while Vern sat nearby, guarding Sigurd and Cory, Sigurd wearing handcuffs Bud had found in Howie's desk. The pair were deeply engrossed in *Lost Treasure* magazines.

Bud was still enjoying the look on Sigurd's face when Wilma Jean had pulled up in her big pink Mary Kay Lincoln Continental and they'd herded the prisoners into the back, Bud deciding he didn't want to pull Howie from what was possibly an evacuation.

He also hadn't been very interested in waiting by the side of the road, so he'd decided he and Vern could guard Sigurd and Cory while his wife drove them to the office, since it wasn't all that far anyway.

Bud now dialed the Radium County Sheriff's Office.

"Radium County Sheriff's Office, Cal Murphy speaking."

"Hey Cal, Bud Shumway. I'm here in the sheriff's office in Green River with Vern Wells. You remember him, don't you?"

"Well, I'll be go to heck," Cal replied. "Of course I remember Vern. Tell him hello for me, will you?"

"Why don't you come on up and tell him yourself? I have some prisoners here that we need you to house for us for awhile, as our sheriff is indisposed, evacuating for a fire and unable to run them over to Castle Dale. I would do it except I don't have the proper vehicle."

"What happened?" Cal asked.

"Well, I have two for armed robbery and accessory, one for possible murder, and maybe two for arson."

"Five? Are you guys having some kind of gang activity over there? I'll need a couple of vehicles."

"No, just two."

"That's what I said, two vehicles," Cal replied.

"No, Cal, just two people."

"Oh. Well, they must be quite the pair."

"Viking stock," Bud replied.

"What? Well, let me check with Hum and see. Are they there with you now?"

"They are."

"Are you able to handle two men by yourself?"

"No, but Vern's here."

"Oh, yeah, sure, sure. Tell him hello. Hang on a minute."

Cal was soon back.

"Bud, we only have one car available until morning."

"Well, OK, that will have to do, seeing how there's only two of them. But I can maybe let one guy out on a personal recognizance, then there will only be one. Surely you can get one guy in the car, right?"

Cal, not realizing that Bud was joking around with him, asked, "You know this accomplice fellow well enough to let him go? He sounds like a handful."

"I do. He actually wasn't much of an accomplice."

"I can take one easily, even two," Cal said. "I'm on my way."

Bud now asked Cory to accompany him outside, where they could talk in private, since the office had only one room. Vern stayed to guard Sigurd, even though he didn't appear to be much of a risk for a getaway at this point.

Bud had gotten the ring back from Sigurd and put it in Howie's safe. He would call the museum when things settled down, probably the next day. He was sure they'd be shocked to learn that the stolen ring from the National Museum of Denmark had ended up in a small town in eastern Utah.

Now outside, leaning against the old brick building, Bud said, "Cory, I don't think I'm going to press charges against you, seeing how you tried to talk Sigurd out of taking the ring and making me walk. I kind of got the feeling you were being railroaded, especially considering your family history with him acting in the role of a father for all those years."

Cory, looking relieved, said, "I really appreciate this, Mr. Shumway, more than you'll ever know. We're leaving tomorrow for California, and I had no idea how I would deal with all this."

"But I still have some unanswered questions I'm hoping you can help me with before Cal gets here and I get sidetracked."

"I'll tell you whatever I can," Cory replied. "But what's going to happen to Sigurd?"

"Well, he'll either plea bargain the charges or go to trial, but I suspect either way he'll enjoy the fine experience of being locked up for awhile, especially when the results from the camp chair come back. I suspect his fingerprints are all over it, as well as Bjorn's blood. If he can convince the judge it was in self-defense, he might get off relatively easy, but given the number of blows to the head, that might be hard to do. Do you have any idea why he tried to make it look like Bjorn was killed by a box of Inuit Pies?"

Cory shook his head. "It was a pretty crazy idea. He told me what had happened, as he wanted me to go help him find the ring. He said he and Bjorn got into a fight over the ring, and Bjorn attacked him. He fought back and killed Bjorn with one of the camp chairs. He then dragged Bjorn into the bushes and frantically tried to figure out a way to make it look like something else had happened. I don't understand why, if it was in self-defense, that he didn't just call the sheriff then and there, except, knowing Sigurd, he'd been drinking."

Bud nodded. "People do odd things when they're scared...and drunk."

Cory continued. "So, the air drop had included a box of Inuit Pies wrapped in dry ice, so he hatched this cockamamie plan to try to make it look like Bjorn had accidentally killed himself by falling off the cliff while trying to kill Erik. Sigurd carried the box of Inuit Pies up onto the cliffs, then dropped it off. He then went back down and carried Bjorn's body out of the bushes and put it by the box so it would look like he'd died there, like he was trying to kill Erik and had instead slipped and fallen and been hit by his own box. He had to make it look like he'd been hit to account for the head wounds, as just falling off the cliff probably wouldn't do that. He back-tracked and erased his tracks from where he carried Bjorn over to the box."

"But why involve Erik?"

"Because Bjorn had a grudge against Erik. Sigurd needed a motive for Bjorn to be up on the cliffs dropping stuff so he could slip and fall and get killed. Remember, he was trying to make it look like Bjorn had accidentally killed himself, but there was really no reason for Bjorn to be up on the cliff."

Cory continued. "See, Erik was going back and forth in the area below, picking up camping gear from the air drop. Bjorn would try to drop the box on him, but instead slip and fall. Sigurd figured everyone would think Bjorn was just being Bjorn. He figured he could get Erik to vouch for him, say he'd been walking back and forth, which he actually had been."

Cory paused, then added, "All this was Sigurd's genius way of making sure people would know why Bjorn dropped the box. Bjorn would be lurking up on the cliff, waiting for the right time to drop the box on Erik's head, and the fact that it was a box with Inuit Bars would emphasize that Bjorn hated Erik and wanted him dead because of the feud. It was supposed to be ironic, I guess."

"So he was trying to think like Bjorn while setting it all up to look like Bjorn did it?" Bud asked.

"Yes, and that included wearing Bjorn's boots while taking the box up the cliff. It would look like Bjorn had been up there, not Sigurd. He told me he even tried to erase the boot tracks as he came back down off the cliff. In the meantime, Erik was over setting up the camp and saw none of this."

"Wow," Bud replied. "Talk about convoluted. It almost seems like Sigurd was losing touch with reality just like Bjorn."

"I'm pretty sure Sigurd was really drunk," Cory replied quietly.

Bud asked, "Do you know more about the ice-cream bar feud?"

"I know more than I wish I did," Cory answered. "My great-grandfather, all on his own, got the idea to make these things he called Sno-Nuts. They were basically an ice-cream bar shaped like a donut, with a hole in the middle. At that point in time, in the 1950s, Inuit Bars had been around since the late 1920s, when Erik's grandfather invented them, and were very successful."

Cory continued. "So, my great-grandfather approached Erik's grandfather to make these Sno-Nuts, as Erik already had the machines set up for the Inuit Bars. Back then, the bigger dairies would lease out the machines and make the product right then and there instead of one company distributing them from a central place, as the shipping was too difficult for frozen products. The dairies would lease the machines and give the company part of their sales proceeds. My grandfather didn't have the money to set up his own machines, so he hoped Inuit Pie would do it for a share of the profit."

Cory paused, then continued. "Well, Inuit Pie said they were interested, but they kept stalling—for two years! Bjorn once showed me a file folder with all the back and forth letters, and Inuit Pie really did lead them on. Then, all of a sudden, Inuit Pie started making Sno-Nuts, though they called them Inuit Pie-Nuts. My great-grandfather took them to court, but he lost. The judge didn't think it was an original enough idea, and Inuit Pie actually had a letter from Eriks' grandfather to one of his employees where he stated that he'd been talking about making a donut-shaped pie for years, asking why he should be interested in buying the idea. I think the way they made my great-grandfather think they were going to work with him was deplorable, but I don't think they stole the idea. Inuit Pie said they'd been reorganizing and that's why they took so long to turn his idea down."

Bud sighed. It all made him glad he ate the stuff straight from the carton.

Cory added, "My dad, Bjorn, knew all this in great detail, but he just couldn't let it go. He thought they'd stolen his inheritance. He threatened to blackmail Erik, though he didn't have anything to blackmail him with. But he sure could be pals with Erik when he needed money or wanted to come along on things like this trip out here for the wedding."

A sheriff's deputy now pulled up in front of the office, and Bud knew it was Cal.

Cory added quietly, "You know, Mr. Shumway, it might be a good thing my dad is dead, because he told me right before the wedding that he was going to flat-out kill Erik."

Bud grimaced, then nodded to Cal as he got out of the vehicle.

Cory added, "And one thing more, we started that fire, but we didn't mean to. It seems to be the Viking motto, 'We didn't mean to,' because that's also what Sigurd said about killing Bjorn. But I know Erik will be good for paying the costs, as he has the money, and he was the one who lit the match. I just hope they put it out soon."

Bud now said goodbye to Cory, who was calling a friend to come get him and go get Sigurd's car, which was still sitting with Bud's FJ on the River Road.

Bud greeted Cal, and they both went inside the Emery County Sheriff's Office, where Vern had now joined Sigurd in reading about lost treasure.

36

Cal left with Sigurd, and Vern's wife came and picked him up, leaving Bud alone at Howie's office. It was late, and Wilma Jean was supposed to come at any time and take Bud out to get his FJ, which was still out on the River Road. He was wishing he could've ridden out with Cory, but he'd had a prisoner at the time and couldn't leave.

Bud now flipped through a *Lost Treasure* magazine, but he'd never been much of a treasure hunter, so he kicked back, put his feet on Howie's desk, and began thinking of all that had happened lately.

It seemed odd to think of Vikings coming to Green River, along with the world's largest steam engine, and Bud still wasn't sure what Howie was up to out at the Rose place and whether or not he would actually be able to grow peanuts. But he did know that Howie's song had been a big hit, and that he and Wilma Jean now owned a big farm, at least on paper. He wondered what the boys were doing and if they were worried he wasn't home yet, as it was definitely getting way past his bedtime.

Before Bud knew it, he was fast asleep and dreaming. He was a Viking, a big and strong man wearing a leather helmet and carrying a big shield with some kind of runes carved into it which supposedly brought happiness to the shield-bearer. He had an axe in one hand

and a spear in the other, and he wore shaggy breeches and had a cloak wrapped around his shoulders.

He turned, and behind him were other Vikings, and he could tell one was Bjorn, his eyes so red they almost glowed. Bud knew he was about to go berserk, and he hoped to stay out of his way. Bjorn sometimes went so mad in battle that he would unknowingly kill his fellow Vikings.

Bud wasn't entirely sure what was going on, but he did know there was some kind of huge dragon that had invaded the country, and he and his fellow Vikings were there waiting for it to come so they could slay it, a tricky proposition, since it was the largest in the land, shoots, maybe in the entire world.

Now he could hear it coming, and its cry made him tremble in fear, as it indeed sounded huge. But he knew he couldn't flee, for he would then be the laughingstock of his kinsmen, and he had high hopes of marrying that most beautiful of Viking women, Griselda Jean or Wimelda Jean or something like that.

And as the dragon approached, blowing smoke from its great nostrils, the dream suddenly changed its point of view and Bud was now a train engineer, wondering what the heck a bunch of men dressed like Vikings were doing on the tracks. He blew the horn and hit the brakes, but...

Bud woke up, startled. It took him awhile to figure out where he was, even after he'd gotten up and walked around some. Where was Wilma Jean? And what a strange dream, though he could see it being the fruit of too much action for a guy who just wanted to sit under a big cottonwood and watch the world go by.

He propped open the office door, letting some fresh air in, then quickly closed it again. The smell of smoke was overpowering, and he could barely make out the street lights through the haze.

It looked like the whole town of Green River was on fire, and he looked up and down the streets to see if he could see anything actually burning. Whatever was going on, he was stuck there, for there was no sign of Wilma Jean.

Just as he was ready to call her, his phone rang, and he could see it was her.

"Yell-ow," he answered.

"Hon, I can't get into town to pick you up. They have Long Street closed because of the fire."

"The fire's clear over there?" Bud asked, knowing Long Street was some distance from the river. And if Long Street was closed, there was no way he could get to the bungalow, as King's Lane connected to Long Street on one end and the other end had been closed the previous day.

"The fire's not over here yet," Wilma Jean said. "They just want to use it for fire access and not have anyone in the way."

"Are you home?" Bud was worried about the dogs.

"Yes, and everything's fine here."

"You left here a long time ago," Bud replied.

"Maureen went home early because she didn't feel well, so I stopped to close up the cafe," she replied. "But I have no idea what's going on with the fire. It was still coming toward town when Vern and I were dropping supplies over there."

"I think I'll walk out and get my FJ," Bud said. "I don't want to be without a vehicle if this fire gets worse. Do you have any idea where Howie is?"

"Maureen called and said she was evacuating and wanted to come to our house, but I told her the road was closed. She asked me the same question about Howie. Where the heck does he hide out half the time lately, anyway?" She sounded upset.

"So where is Maureen going?"

"Over to Krider's house. She can stay downstairs with Kale and Molly. The people staying upstairs are leaving tomorrow."

Bud had forgotten what Wilma Jean had said about the house being rented. He now wondered if Cory and the wedding party were there. He worried about it being in the path of the fire, and wondered where everyone would go if they had to evacuate.

"Is this the same people from California who were there before?" He asked.

"It is," she replied.

"I think I can get one of them to take me out to get my FJ," Bud said.

"You know them?"

"One of them," Bud replied. "I'll let you know what's going on when I know."

He hung up, dug Cory's phone number from his pocket, then called him. Before Bud knew it, he and Cory were on their way to get Bud's FJ, car windows up to keep the smoke out.

37

"Sheriff, I really appreciate you picking me up last night," Howie said, feet up on his desk. "I don't know what I would've done without you."

"Howie, you're just lucky I was able to get over there, since you'd blocked off all the streets. I had a hunch something was wrong when nobody could get through to you on the phone, especially Maureen."

Bud didn't want to tell Howie what his real thoughts had been, how he'd wondered if he weren't out at the Rose Ranch. Instead, after getting his FJ, he'd decided to go to Howie's house and look for him, driving around the barricades.

"I can't believe I left my phone in the rig," Howie said. "I'm tired, but I need to get back over there. As of 5 a.m., when I last talked to fire dispatch, everything was still out of control and burning clear up to the edge of the golf course. The fire had laid down some during the night, but it was starting to wake up again. A few hundred feet more, and my house is toast. And if the old railroad bridge burns, there won't be any trains coming through for awhile."

"The bridge is steel, Howie, but a fire would for sure shut it down until they could inspect everything. But I'm just glad to know you're OK. We were all worried about you. You need to get some rest. Go on over to Krider's and I'll cover for you."

"Thanks, maybe I should. But I don't understand it, Bud. I told Maureen what I was doing, but she didn't seem to register it at all. She went ahead and evacuated everything without me, and I was just over in the field looking for that little white bunny. No way was I going to let it burn up."

He nodded toward the little rabbit in a nearby box of hay, eating strawberries. Bud wished he could tell Howie that Maureen was pregnant and probably not her usual self, but he'd promised her he wouldn't say a word. It was getting tiresome, though. Maybe she was going to wait and tell Howie after the baby was born, Bud mused. After all, she was starting to show, and everyone in town knew about it except its dad.

It was dawn, and neither Bud nor Howie had gotten any sleep the previous night. Fire dispatch had called and said they needed to evacuate the neighborhood behind Howie's, over where Sherwyn lived, so they'd been out all night helping people get their animals and possessions out. One guy had several mules that they'd had to load and take over to the ballpark, where a temporary corral had been set up.

"I'm just going to lay my head down here on the desk for a few minutes, Bud. Wake me up if anything happens."

Howie was soon fast asleep.

Now Bud thought he could hear an airplane, so he went out to take a look. The smoke wasn't nearly as bad as it had been, and he could now see in the early light what looked to be two military-type planes coming in from the north. They looked to Bud like tanker planes.

Bud watched as the planes got closer and closer, losing altitude, until they turned and swung directly over the river in the direction of Howie's house. He could see red fire retardant drop as each plane took its turn flying low over the fire.

"Howie, wake up!" Bud shook Howie, but he was in a deep sleep and didn't respond.

Bud made sure the little bunny couldn't get out, then wrapped Howie's jacket into a ball and put it under his head as a makeshift pillow. He'd go on over to fire headquarters at the grade school and let Howie sleep.

He got there just as breakfast was being served, and since he was representing the sheriff's office, they invited him to eat with them. Bud thought he had a healthy appetite, but he'd never seen anyone wolf down food like the hotshot crews. If even one crew would move to Green River, Wilma Jean would get rich, he thought.

As Bud sat talking to a young hotshot from Idaho, the mayor of Green River, Rich, saw him and stopped by.

"Say, Bud, could I have a word with you when you get a minute?"

Bud excused himself and went over to a corner table where the mayor sat alone, frowning.

"Bud, this is just between you and me and the bedpost, OK?"

Bud wondered what was going on.

"I just got handed a resignation letter yesterday afternoon from Sheriff McPherson. Bud, Howie says he won't be able to keep up with being sheriff and running his drive-in at the same time. I asked him about Maureen, but he says she's already too busy managing your wife's cafe. He says something's got to give, that he's stretched too thin and needs to ease off a little. He highly recommended I offer you the position."

Bud grinned.

"I get it, Bud," Rich smiled. "It's ironic, for sure, for you to have hired Howie as your deputy when you were sheriff, then you recommended Howie as sheriff when you resigned, and now it's all reversed."

Bud found it interesting, for sure. As Rich talked, Bud wondered if part of the reason Howie was so busy was someone named Cassie Rose. He then immediately felt guilty—he was hanging Howie without even giving him a trial. There had to be something else going on, but Bud couldn't figure what it would be.

Bud asked, "When's his last day?"

The mayor answered, "He says he'll stay on until you can start, whatever that takes."

Bud laughed. "Nothing like a little pressure. But you do know we just bought the Krider farm."

The mayor looked surprised. "No, I didn't know that. Sounds like you may already have a full-time job, though I thought the winters were pretty slow for farmers."

"Actually, Rich, they are," Bud replied. "To be honest, I sometimes get kind of bored. But I'm also really getting into my photography and was planning on doing more of that this winter."

Rich said, "Bud, I remember when you resigned from the force. That was a really bad day for me. None of us thought Howie could do the job, but with your mentoring, he's turned out just fine. It would make up for that bad day I had back then if you would say yes here today. I'd be more than willing to have you work as many hours as you need to run things, then back off and do whatever you want when things are slow. You'd be on salary, so no need to keep track of hours either way. But remember, this is Green River, Utah, for cryin' out loud. This fire is a rarity. Nothing ever happens here."

Bud was quiet for a long time, and he knew Rich was expecting him to say no.

Finally, he replied, "Rich, hows about a deal like this. Howie's going to find that, like the farm, his drive-in is slower in the winter. There will be times he'll be having trouble making ends meet financially, especially with this new...whoops, it's a secret..."

"Baby?" Rich asked. "Everybody in town knows they're having a baby except Howie. You know how word gets out around here."

Bud laughed. "He'll be busy with that little one. I guess if it's a boy they're naming him Malcolm."

"You mean Maureen's naming him Malcolm. Howie's not even aware he exists yet."

"Anyway," Bud continued. "I was thinking that Howie could be my deputy again, though just part-time, and do like you're offering me, work when we have things going on, then spend his time in the drive-in when he needs to."

"What about an emergency situation, like what we've got going on now?" Rich asked, nodding at the firefighters around them.

Bud asked, "Say, where did the money for air tankers come from, anyway?"

Rich said, "Some guy named Erik Nelson. He came to me and offered to pay whatever we needed to get this fire out. His family used to live here, so I guess he has a connection somehow."

"They used to own the Krider farm. He's president of the Inuit Pie Company."

"Well, that's good to know. I guess he can afford to help out."

Bud decided not to mention Erik's role in starting the fire. He continued, "Rich, I have an assistant out at the farm, and I believe he would like to go from half-time to full-time. Farming's starting to take its toll on my body, and if I were on an as-needed basis on the farm, it would make things easier. And Howie can always get someone to back him up if need be, even my wife or Maureen if they're not busy, though that's unlikely."

"Does this mean yes?" Rich asked, his eyes lighting up.

"I think I could do a good job, make a good sheriff for you and the townspeople," Bud replied quietly.

Rich grinned, shaking Bud's hand, and as Bud turned to go, he added, "Bud, you'll always be sheriff here, you know that."

Bud just nodded his head, his eyes filled with tears—probably from all the smoke, he figured.

As Bud walked out the door, Rich added, "And Sherwyn says he wants you to return that grocery cart you've been carrying around in the back of your FJ."

38

The fire was finally out, the Vikings had left town, and Bud finally felt like he could relax and enjoy what was left of autumn before the cold weather hit.

He'd gone over to the golf course at the state park to look at an old riding mower they had for sale, hoping to get something that would make cutting the grass at the bungalow an easier chore next summer.

He'd met up with the state park manager and taken the mower for a test run, cruising along the edge of the fairway, then had decided to buy it. He was just leaving to go get the farm pickup to haul it when he saw Howie, presumably on his way home.

Seeing Bud, Howie pulled over and got out, leaning on Bud's FJ.

"Sheriff, do I ever have some good news!" Howie said excitedly. "A star is born!"

Bud, figuring Maureen had finally told Howie about the baby, said, "Don't you mean *will be* born?"

"Well, OK, technically it's not a star, but I have the paperwork here. It's official."

Bud was puzzled, "So Maureen showed you the results of the test?"

Howie said, "Test? Bud, whatever you do, don't tell Maureen. It's got to be kept a secret until I decide the best time."

Bud sighed. As usual, he and Howie were on different pages, probably not even in the same book this time.

"OK, Howie," Bud replied. "I won't say a word. I'm not sure what I'm supposed to be keeping a secret, but if I ever figure it out, it's just between you and me."

"You'll know when the time's right," Howie replied. "But this means I can get back to working on the drive-in, though I'd much rather be out at Cassie's."

"Roger that," Bud said, not knowing what else to say.

He was feeling rather put-off with Howie, not just for going out on Maureen, but also for having no compunctions about it. But at least Howie was being honest, Bud thought, even though he didn't want Maureen to know.

"You know, Howie, Maureen called me the other day. What do you think of the name Malcolm?"

"I dunno Bud, it's a nice enough name, but what does it have to do with Maureen?"

Maureen had called Bud to see if he liked the name, and he had, but he was beginning to feel like a surrogate father and wished she'd tell Howie.

"Howie, you need to spend some time with your wife. She's got a lot on her plate right now."

This would make yet another sentence lately that Bud instantly wished he could retract. He added, "I'm sorry. It's not my place to tell you how to live, especially since you didn't even ask."

"It's OK, Sheriff," Howie said. "I know I haven't been home much, with the fire and this Big Boy thing and trying to get the drive-in ready, but she's never home, either."

"And with your evening activities..." Bud added.

Once again, Howie never missed a beat. "Right, but that's about over now. I've satisfied my curiosity big time with this one, Bud. It's amazing how much of your time something like this can take."

Bud groaned. How could Howie be so insensitive and blasé about something so serious?

Howie added, "Cassie will be back tomorrow. I need to go take care of her cat one last time and pick up my telescope and camera."

Bud was speechless. Cat? Telescope? Camera?

"I guess I might as well tell you, Bud, but don't tell anyone. They're coming to town for a big ceremony, and I want it to be a big surprise for Maureen."

Bud's head was spinning. "Who's coming to town?"

"The people from the Minor Planet Center. I just discovered a new comet, something even the professional astronomers didn't see coming. It's a really unique one, as it appears to have a gas tail, and most are made of ice. It takes a long time to track something like that, Bud, as well as figure out things like its magnitude and declination and path."

"As discoverer, I got to name it, though normally it would be named my last name, McPherson. But I named it after Maureen—Comet Maureen, officially C/2019 Maureen."

"Cassie's roof is the perfect observatory—it's really dark out there. I've also been taking care of her cat while she went back home to Michigan for a few months, since I was out there anyway. Looking through a telescope for hours wasn't easy, but Bud, it was worth it."

"Comet Maureen?" Bud asked.

"She's the love of my life, and this comet will carry her name forever, or at least until it crashes into the sun, as comets are known to do."

Bud shook his head in disbelief.

"Oh, and Sheriff, one more thing…"

"What's that, Howie?"

"I resigned as sheriff."

Bud quietly said, "I know. Rich told me. He offered me the job, just like you recommended."

"Are you going to take it?"

"I am, Howie."

Bud and Howie high-fived each other, and Bud started his FJ and drove back to the farm, feeling like he was in a dream.

Somehow, he knew Maureen would soon tell Howie about the baby, and in due time, he would ask Howie if he wanted to be his deputy again.

39

Bud leaned against his FJ, playing stick with the dogs, waiting for Wilma Jean, Vern, and Howie to show up. He was parked next to the almost-dry Muddy Creek, and he could see Hondu Arch high above, shaped like the small loop on a saddle that holds a cowboy's rope in place.

A small grove of huge Fremont cottonwoods stood nearby, and beneath it sat several camp chairs, two of which held Maureen and Vern's wife, Iris. They appeared to be talking about little Malcolm, for Iris would lean over every once in awhile to pat Maureen's tummy. Bud knew Iris had several grandchildren and doted on them and would be a good mentor for Maureen.

Bud now pulled a small harmonica from his pocket and begin fiddling with it, blowing into one side, then turning it over and blowing into the other. He'd found it over at the grade school when he'd had breakfast with the hotshot crews. He could already almost play *Red River Valley*, and he decided this was the best fiddling device ever, since he could not only fiddle with it, but actually play it.

The dogs were now down in the small creek, splashing around, though Bud wasn't sure how it even qualified as a creek, since it was only a few feet wide and maybe a foot deep. But he knew that during the monsoon season, this little rivulet could turn into a raging river, especially on down a ways, where it had created a deep slot canyon known as the Chute of Muddy Creek.

It was on beyond the Chute and where Muddy Creek actually exited the San Rafael Reef that Vern's grandfather had landed his small plane in a feat that had become part of canyon lore and mythology.

It was a beautiful bluebird day, the deep-blue sky making the leaves of the golden cottonwoods stand out like gold filagree against a cloak of royal color. Bud had already taken a bunch of photos, and from what he could see on his LED screen, they looked to be outstanding. He especially liked the one of Hondu Arch framed by old gnarly cottonwood trunks.

He'd also taken several photos of the boys playing in the water and chasing sticks, which he would add to his collection of hundreds —maybe thousands—of dog photos.

Maybe he should become a dog photographer, Bud mused, smiling at the thought. He could make calendars of dog photos for animal lovers, using the canyons and cliffs of the Big Empty for back-grounds.

He'd have to get a bunch more dogs for variety, but now that they had the big farm, there would be plenty of room for all. He could get a little trailer to pull behind the FJ, and they could convert the equip-ment shed to kennels, though he knew that would be useless, as everyone would want to pile on the bed with him and Wilma Jean.

Now again fiddling with the harmonica, Bud thought of his conversation a few days ago with Mayor Rich, and he felt pleased with the outcome.

In a way, it would be the best of both worlds, for when things got slow at the sheriff's office, he could swing by the house, get the boys, and go check things on the farm, maybe even taking time to sit under the big cottonwood and play stick.

And he could still park at the bungalow with his FJ heading out, as he might need to make a fast getaway now and then, though he'd have to be careful to not spray Wilma Jean's petunias with gravel.

Howie had accepted his offer to become part-time deputy, laughing and saying something about how things always stay the same, no matter how much they change. Bud knew that Howie had been conflicted about quitting as sheriff, and this seemed to be the best of both worlds for him, also.

Bud now looked to the sky, expecting to see Wilma Jean's bright pink Cessna Skyhawk at any minute. He knew Vern and Howie would be with her.

Maureen and Iris had come with Bud in his FJ and had already spread the picnic out on a camp table under the trees.

But thought he could hear his stomach growling and wished he'd had more than a snack before leaving Green River, but the growling soon turned into something he'd heard only a few times before, and never out in the canyons.

Far in the distance, barely audible, came a mournful sound that made him think of faraway places and distant horizons and his Uncle Junior.

It was Union Pacific's Big Boy Engine 4014, returning from Ogden to Cheyenne by the southern route, and Bud knew it would stop in Green River for only an hour or so, then continue on its journey.

For a moment, he felt that same wanderlust he'd felt as a kid when he'd run off to work for the Musser boys. This in turn made him think of the Viking ring that he'd been privileged to hold up to the setting sun, reading a message from an unknown metalsmith of a thousand years past.

He wondered for a moment where all the Vikings were—Erik and Cory and Liz and John—and he figured they were back in California, getting on with their lives—all but Sigurd, that is, who was currently housed in the Castle Dale Courthouse jail and who looked to soon be going to prison up in Draper, near Salt Lake City.

As the train whistle faded into the distance, it was replaced with the hum of an airplane engine, and seeing a pink plane above, Bud knew that Wilma Jean and the crew would soon be landing.

They'd originally planned on going to the backcountry airstrip just over the hill at the Hidden Splendor Mine, but Bud had heard from his old-timer friends Eldon Daddage and Frosty Merriott that the road had been washed out with this last big storm that had come through. Eldon and Frosty spent half their time out in the backcountry, so Bud knew if they said it was impassible, it definitely was.

There was no airstrip at Hondu, but Bud had checked out the road, and it was in fine shape for a backcountry landing. This was remote-enough country that there was no traffic, especially this time of year.

The plane was now overhead, and he knew the pilot was scoping everything out. He hoped that Vern was on the stick, given all his backcountry experience, but knowing his wife, he suspected she was flying the plane.

The plane turned and flew back toward the cliffs, which were dotted with dog-leg uranium mines from the boom times of the 1950s and 60s. It then turned again, all the time losing altitude.

Bud held his breath as the Cessna finally sat down, raising puffs of dust when the pilot applied the brakes. It soon rolled to a stop, not far from the cottonwood grove, where Maureen and Iris were now standing, maybe to see better or maybe to be ready to run, Bud smiled. He was now happy, knowing everyone was safe.

Vern got out of the passenger seat, and Bud knew then that his wife had made that landing, smooth as butter, just like a pro. Now Howie got out of the back and went over to Maureen, putting his arm around her, and Bud wondered when the comet ceremony would be.

Wilma Jean got out last, and as she stood by the plane, her hand shading her eyes as she surveyed the scene, Bud managed to take what he knew would become a classic photo of her against the bright pink plane and the blue sky, with the words, "Cessna Cafe," shining like stars in the night.

Bud again started playing his rough rendition of *Red River Valley* as Wilma Jean walked toward him, smiling, the dogs running to her.

And Bud knew something special was there before him at that moment in time, right there—that blue sky, the red cliffs, the slow flow of Muddy Creek, the golden trees, his friends, the dogs, his wife —and even that bright pink plane.

Like the Vikings with their North Star, Bud knew he was looking at the secret to happiness, and he knew it really wasn't much of a secret after all.

And he knew he would never need or want anything more.

———

ABOUT THE AUTHOR

Chinle Miller writes from southeastern Utah and western Colorado, where she spends most of her time wandering with her dogs. She has an A.S. in Geology, a B.A. in Anthropology and an M.A. in Linguistics.

If you enjoyed this book, you'll also enjoy the other books in the Bud Shumway mystery series:

The Ghost Rock Cafe
The Slickrock Cafe
The Paradox Cafe
The No Delay Cafe
The Silver Spur Cafe
The Ice House Cafe
The Rattlesnake Cafe
The Beartooth Cafe
The Melon Rind Cafe
The Cessna Cafe
The Klondike Cafe
The Yellow Cat Cafe
The Swiftcurrent Cafe
The Sunnyside Cafe
The Temple Mountain Cafe

And don't miss *Desert Rats: Adventures in the American Outback, Uranium Daughter, Wandering off the Map,* and *The Impossibility of Loneliness,* also by Chinle Miller.

And if you enjoy Bigfoot stories, you'll love *Rusty Wilson's Bigfoot Campfire Stories* and his many other Bigfoot books, as well as his popular *Chasing After Bigfoot: My Search for North America's Most Elusive Creature*.

Other offerings from Yellow Cat Publishing include an RV series by RV expert Sunny Skye, which includes *Living the Simple RV Life, The Truth about the RV Life,* and *RVing with Pets,* as well as *Tales of a Campground Host*. And don't forget to check out the books by Sunny's friend, Bob Davidson: *On the Road with Joe* and *Any Road, USA*. And finally, you'll love Roger Dean Miller's comedy thriller, *Bombing Hoffman*.

www.ingramcontent.com/pod-product-compliance
Lightning Source LLC
Chambersburg PA
CBHW031111260626
47172CB00001B/316